Robin L Baccile
Peter M Baccile

Books by Jane O'Brien

The White Pine Trilogy:
The Tangled Roots of Bent Pine Lodge #1
The Dunes & Don'ts Antiques Emporium #2
The Kindred Spirit Bed & Breakfast #3

The Lighthouse Trilogy:
The 13th Lighthouse #1
The Painted Duck #2
Owl Creek #3

The Unforgettables:
Ruby and Sal #1
Maisy and Max #2

Maisy and Max

Connect with Jane O'Brien

www.authorjaneobrien.com

http://www.amazon.com/author/obrienjane

www.facebook.com/janeobrien/author/

Contact: authorjaneobrien@gmail.com

7

Vaudeville is dead. The acrobats, the animal acts, the dancers, the singers, and the old-time comedians have taken their final bows and disappeared into the wings of obscurity. For fifty years--from 1875 to 1925--vaudeville was the popular entertainment of the masses. Nomadic tribes of nondescript players roamed the land. The vaudeville actor was part gypsy and part suitcase. With his brash manner, flashy clothes, capes and cane, and accompanied by his gaudy womenfolk, the vaudevillian brought happiness and excitement to the communities he visited.

FRED ALLEN, Much Ado About Me

Maisy and Max

Table of Contents

Prologue – London, 1889 – 1890

Edward was eager to leave London. The circus had been here almost two months, since the beginning of November, and even though the weather had been a little more agreeable the last few days, it was still cold and damp. He was told the temperatures would continue to climb away from the 5-7 degrees Celsius it had been hovering at, but numbers didn't really matter when you were cold. Cold was cold. He was looking forward to the crossing to New York, and then Barnum & Bailey would take its winter break in Connecticut, before starting on their scheduled route again in April. Edward didn't usually mind traveling, but this year it had been wearing on him a little more than it usually did at the end of the season. The extended months for the European tour had been difficult. Maybe it was because he was without a mate. A nice woman would have done wonders to keep him warm at night, and the companionship would have been a whole lot better than the roustabouts he usually chummed with. The simple fact was that Edward was growing older and ready to settle down, something he never would have thought about himself in a million years.

A walk in the rain was probably a bad idea, but Edward needed some time alone. He had to think about his future and ponder what was to become of him if he ever left the circus life. He roamed from street to street, each one more dismal than the last. London was a dark and dreary place in the 1890s, especially for the poor.

He stopped for a minute to look around and get his bearings, trying to decide if he was lost, when a shop window decorated with brightly colored scarves caught his eye. The festivity reminded him of the vivid circus colors meant to attract attention. He crossed the street to see what it was about, and as he drew near he could read the letters painted on the glass -- *Fortune Telling. See Your Future.* Edward smiled to himself because they had the same type of fortune tellers in the circus, and he knew they were all a sham. He had been in on some of the shake downs himself, helping poor souls who only wanted some predictions to feel better about themselves. Some marks were more difficult than others, but they all caved eventually. Out of curiosity as to how they did things here in England, he entered. His experience would be good for a laugh when he retold it back at the grounds.

A small bell tinkled when he opened the door, and shortly after a striking woman dressed in a turban and a long loose kaftan came to greet him. Her makeup was exaggerated, and she wore an excess of jewelry –

huge gold hoops in her ears, and several necklaces around her neck. The colors of the gems flashed in the dim light from the exposed bulbs hanging overhead. Her expression was blank as she beckoned him to come behind the curtain of beads; the bracelets on her wrist clinked pleasantly with the movement of her hand. Edward smiled to himself when he saw the traditional crystal globe on the table; a burning taper beside it dripped wax on the cloth. It was exactly the way the circus fortune teller was set up; it was all too familiar, but when he sat down across from her, he felt the hair on his arms stand up.

"So, you want to know your fortune?" she asked in a sultry tone, as she leaned forward and stared directly into his eyes.

"Uh, yes," said Edward. He was a little shaken, and he had no idea why -- he knew the drill. "I am trying to make a decision, and I thought I could use some help."

There was silence as she studied him, making him feel very uncomfortable. "You want a mate?" she asked in her thick accent. "Yes, I can see it clearly."

Edward wondered if she was trying to sell herself to him. He turned a deep shade of red. She laughed making him feel embarrassed; he was not an innocent child; he had had experiences – just not any kind of permanent relationship. "Yes, actually," he stuttered. "Perhaps, I *am* looking for a wife."

She smiled for the first time. "Now we are getting somewhere. Give me your hands." Edward reached across the table and took both of her hands in his – she gasped, and pulled back.

"What? What happened?" he asked.

"I think you are a very special man. I think you are the one I have been waiting for."

"What do you mean?"

She reached up to her neck and unclasped what looked like a ruby and diamond necklace, but as he well knew, it was most likely the same kind of fake paste that all the circus performers wore. She wrapped it around her fingers and closed her eyes, then she took his hands into hers once again, with the necklace touching them both. Edward felt a warmth and tingle right down to his toes. He smiled, relaxed, and closed his eyes; it felt like home; it felt like comfort; it felt like love.

"What is your name?" she softly asked.

"Edward. Edward Woods."

Her eyes widened. "You are Gypsy? You speak Romani?"

"No, I don't speak Romani, but I have been told that my ancestors are Romani from Wales."

"Of course you are. So I thought. Here, take this." She separated her hands from his and pushed the necklace into his hands alone.

"Why?" Edward was completely puzzled. He had come here for a reading, not a piece of jewelry.

"This necklace has special powers. It has been waiting many years for you. It wants to be with you and you only. It will bring you the answers you need, and when you know the time is right, you will pass it on to the one you love and receive wondrous results." Then she smiled a very seductive smile. "Would you like to try it out?"

Edward did not have a clue what she was talking about, and beautiful as she was, he had no intention of doing what he was sure she was suggesting. Besides he couldn't afford to buy the necklace, anyway. After last night's card game, he was flat broke.

She laughed out loud as she read his mind. "No, there is no need to pay me for the bauble. It is yours, as it should be. I have only been the caretaker. It is my pleasure to find the rightful owner. Now, go and find your woman; she will be much more eager than I."

Present Day, 2017

Chapter One

Ivy wasn't used to attending events of this sort by herself. She felt a little lonely with no one to talk to – a little out of place. Before settling into her plush theater seat at the end of the aisle, she stopped a moment to take in the beauty of the Frauenthal Theater. The brochure pointed out that it was originally called The Michigan Theater and was built here in Muskegon in 1929. It proclaimed itself to be a theater that showed "100% all talking pictures." A few years ago, there had been a big drive to save the theater, and as soon as the renovations were completed, it became the pride of the city. Not one thing had been changed that would take away from its beauty, from the heavy velvet drapes, to the ornate ceiling, and the large carving over the stage. She could almost taste the excitement of the theatergoers in the twenties when "talkies" were a new and exciting pastime. And here she was, now, experiencing her first Buster Keaton movie at the International Film Festival that was held every fall in his honor. Buster's family owned a cottage on Muskegon Lake and because he had spent many of his childhood to young adult summers here, he had always called Muskegon his home. A bronze statue of Buster looking through a hand crank movie camera on a tripod had been placed near the front entrance as a testament to his skills as a director.

Having spent so much of the past few years in the small town of Whitehall watching over her grandmothers at the nursing home, Ivy had almost forgotten what it was like to be a free adult with no responsibilities. Attending this event was a real luxury and one she intended to enjoy to the fullest, even though she *was* actually working. Her book 'Ruby and Sal' had done much better than the publisher had expected; sales continued to climb on a daily basis, and there were hopes that soon she would reach the New

York Times Best Seller List. Ivy was thrilled and more than a little awed at what had happened to her life. As a result of her success, her publisher had asked her to start on another book that they might consider publishing next. The subject of prohibition, Al Capone, and bootlegging had been well-received, so in the spirit of that era, Ivy had begun to research what other 'Unforgettables', as her great-grandmother Ruby had called them, might be connected to West Michigan, which was Ivy's area of the state. She was surprised to find how many famous and infamous people were either from this state or had a connection in some way. When she came across information about The Keatons, she dove head on into the research, and now here she was, getting ready to see her first silent film on the big screen, complete with live organ accompaniment. She only wished she had someone with her to share it with, to lean into and whisper a comment or critique.

≈

It had been over a year since she had last seen or heard from Fox Marzetti. In the short time she had known him, they had already become a couple in her mind. She had thought of him as the love of her life – the one she was meant to be with. After all, her ruby scarf had entangled them, his car was named Ruby, her great-grandmother was named Ruby, and he had a love of the prohibition era. So many coincidences! Then after what she felt was the ultimate betrayal when he had bid on her great-grandmother Ruby's home and won, knowing full well what that house meant to her, she had made a vow never to speak to him again. From that experience she had learned to hold her emotions in check. She would no longer allow herself to move so quickly in a relationship as she had with Fox; the pain was too great when that relationship was no more. The emptiness left behind was a void she couldn't bear to live through again. She had had too much disappointment and grief in her life already.

But suddenly someone new had come into her life, and it was as if a ray of sunshine had surrounded her entire body, leaving her warm and cozy from her head to her toes, and she knew her life would never be the same. And even though he wasn't with her tonight, she could bear the loneliness for a few hours, because she knew without a shadow of a doubt, he would always be there for her and she would never be alone again. It was a wonderful feeling that she had not known was possible, and it filled her like no other had ever done before, because they would be a part of each other's life for all of eternity – she was certain of it. Ivy sighed with joy whenever she thought of his handsome face, laughing with her, sometimes crying with her, but always and ever with her, in her heart and in her spirit. She glanced at her cell phone wondering if there was a text of some kind that would need her attention before the show began. Yes, apparently she had missed the alert sound when she had turned her phone to vibrate. The simple message read, *"All is well. Down for the night. Take your time. Enjoy yourself."*

Knowing that everything was fine at home allowed her to relax, so she was ready to settle in and begin the movie. With notebook and pen in hand, she planned to scribble notes the best she could in the dark as she viewed 'The General,' one of Buster's most famous movies of the silent film era, and considered one of the greatest American films ever made. It tells of a true Civil War event known as The Great Locomotive Chase, which was a train chase between the Union Army and the Confederates through the mountains of Georgia and Tennessee, ending in Chattanooga. Buster chose to make the story into a comedy, which was not a good choice for the time period. Films were new and the people less sophisticated in their comedy viewing. Buster overran his budget, by purchasing three Civil War era trains, building actual bridges for the sole purpose of blowing them up, and making dams to increase the depth of the streams and rivers. At a final cost of $750,000, 'The General' became the most expensive silent film ever produced. After completing 'The General,' he was forced to sign a strict contract with MGM, so that the studio could keep his spending under control.

Reading her brochure, Ivy discovered that 'The General' was a box office flop in 1926 because the majority of people did not find anything funny about killing soldiers, but in later days the film would be viewed through different eyes and has since been listed number 8 in the list of the best films ever made in America. Ivy had already viewed the film on DVD, but she hoped the large screen and live music would add a new dimension, and give her more insight into her newest book venture.

"Excuse me, dear. Do you mind if I sit next to you?"

"What? Oh, no, sorry. Go ahead. I'm not expecting anyone. Here, let me move over one seat." Ivy glanced up from her reading, and looked into the eyes of a very old woman. She was using a cane, which she leaned on to support herself, as she lowered herself slowly into her seat. She was short and frail, but her height was probably due to the fact that she was quite bent over – most likely from osteoarthritis. Ivy noticed that her hands were gnarled and some of her fingers were curled in toward her palms. Her clothes were loose and flowing, and she had adorned herself with several necklaces and a pair of huge hoop earrings, giving her a gypsy look, similar to what children wore when dressing up on Halloween.

"Thank you. I don't really like to sit alone, but I have no choice most times, now; do I?" She chuckled, and as she did so, her face created a map of wrinkles, some grooves so deep they reminded Ivy of winding rivers at the base of a gorge.

"Is this your first time to the film festival?" asked Ivy, trying to make polite conversation with the woman.

"Oh no, dear; I come every year. I have a love for Buster -- always have. And you? First time?"

"Yes, it is. I'm quite excited."

"I see your notebook and pen. Are you a student?" she asked

Ivy laughed. "No, I'm way past student material."

"Well, you're never too old to learn," the old woman said. She reached over and patted Ivy's hand, and a warmth radiated through her to her core. "So why the notetaking, then?"

Ivy gasped and gingerly pulled her hand back, so as not to offend her seating partner. "I'm writing a book, actually, and I need to do some research of this time period in Muskegon."

"Oh my, what a wonderful hobby."

"Well, it's not really a hobby, anymore. I was recently published, and now my agent is requesting another story to follow up with the last," said Ivy, proudly.

The woman's face lit up. "Are you, by any chance, that Ivy Morton, who wrote Ruby and Sal?"

"Why, yes, I am. How would you know that?"

"I know things. I always have. It's a gift, you could say." As she gestured the bangles on her wrists jingled softly. Her long hair, which must have been glorious when she was young, hung down her back in a wispy cloud of white. When she turned her head to look at Ivy, her gold hoop earrings flashed brightly, even though the theater lights had dimmed. "I loved your story of Ruby and Sal. You have a way with words. That is *your* gift."

"You mean you've actually read it?" Ivy was amazed. The only comments she had ever received were from friends and family. She had never met a stranger who had read Ruby and Sal. This was so strange, that this woman would sit next to *her*, of all the people in the theater.

"Not only did I read it, but I loved it! And I can't wait to see what you have in store for me to read next."

"Thank you, thank you so much -- I'm sorry, I didn't get your name. I guess I should know who my fans are; right?"

"My name is not important, dear. But I feel the need to tell you that you must get your life on track, Ivy. We are on this Earth such a short time. Don't waste a minute."

"What do you mean? My life is perfect. I like my life. And what would you know about my life, anyway?" At first Ivy was upset with the audacity of this woman.

But she could see that she meant no harm. There was a kindness and gentleness about her. She was just a lonely old woman who had delusions of being a fortune teller. She decided it was best to play it safe and keep this irrational woman happy.

"Well, I know you don't believe me, but I know that you have left something unsettled," she went on. "Something that bothers you in the night; someone that comes to your dreams and makes you cry out with the loss. You must fix it, and soon, before it's too late."

Ivy could barely breathe. How did she know these things? How could she know that Ivy would wake up in a sweat, shaking, feeling as though she had lost the most important thing in her life? The only way she had found to quell the feelings were to quietly chant to herself, 'I'm happy. I'm fulfilled. I'm loved and I love.' And then she would tuck in her legs and wrap her arms around her midriff, and rock herself back to sleep. No one knew this. Not even Nancy. It was impossible that this stranger could see into her soul.

The organ music began to play as the lights grew darker. The woman leaned over again and handed Ivy a business card. "Contact this person. She has information you can use for your story." When Ivy's fingers touched her contorted hand, an electrical shock ran up her arm and straight to her heart. For a moment she actually thought the beating had stopped, but it had only skipped a beat or two, and then as soon as the touch was over, her heart went back to its normal rhythm.

Ivy watched in a daze, as the woman slowly raised herself up. "Do as I say, child, and your life will be full and happy." She stared a moment at Ivy, nodded her head in a silent goodbye, and shuffled up the aisle just as the curtain opened and the black and white film began to flicker on the screen.

Chapter Two

The crowds slowly moved out of the theater into the gorgeous October night; many people were dressed in their finest 1920s garb, featuring feathers, gloves, spats, and suspenders. Now that the screening was over, people were eagerly talking to each other about the antics of Buster Keaton. 'Can you believe that scene where he sits on the cross piece between the train wheels and rides it into a tunnel as the engine begins to move?' Ivy heard someone say. 'Oh yes, and what about that scene where the bridge collapses and the train falls into a river? That was a real train. Amazing!'

Even though she had watched this film several times already, it always amazed her when she thought of the fact that there was no CGI back then; what you saw is what actually took place. At this stage in the movies they had not yet figured out how to deceive the audience. The actors were their own stunt doubles – Ivy wasn't even sure if that term had even been invented at this time in the early 1920s. How did Buster jump from moving train cars so nimbly and then fall without getting hurt? He was truly amazing. Every move was perfectly calculated and rehearsed, and still it seemed as though it was happening completely by accident. Yes, this was the man she needed to write about in her next book, but what could she say that had not already been said? Buster Keaton's life was an open book.

"Miss! Excuse me. Oops, pardon me. Wait up, miss, you dropped your phone."

Ivy felt someone tap her on the back and upon turning around, she came face-to-face with a young woman about her age, who was holding up a phone. She was shorter than Ivy, with dark curly hair framing her pleasantly round face. She seemed like the kind of person who had never met a stranger.

"Oh, my, that looks like mine. It's the same case, anyway. Thank you so much. Let me take a look inside to make sure." As Ivy flipped open the leather case with the magnetic enclosure, the slots meant for business cards or a driver's license was exposed. "Yep, it's mine, all right."

"Oh good, I'm so glad I caught you," she said. "I noticed it in the aisle near the row you had exited."

"I'm glad you saw it. Thank you." Ivy laughed. "How can we live without these things?"

When the woman caught a look at the interior of the case, she gasped in surprise, and said, "Might I ask how you got my card?"

"What do you mean?

"I spotted my card in your case, there. I'm Veronica Woods Darnell, and that's my business card."

"Really?" asked Ivy in surprise. "I was given this card just this evening by a woman who was sitting next to me. She said I would need to talk to you about something. It was all very mysterious. I'm not sure what she meant."

"Uh, was she short with long white hair and dressed like a gypsy?"

"Why, yes she was. She sort of spoke in riddle to me. I didn't know what to make of her."

"Oh, dear." The woman turned a light shade of pale. "Oh, my. I can't believe it came true."

"What do you mean?"

"I think I'd better tell you about myself and see what Gina had in mind."

"Gina?"

"Yes, that's the only name I know her by. She approached me last year and – Would you like to get some coffee? We have to talk."

"I guess I have a few minutes, but not a lot of time. It's been a long day, and I'd like to get home."

"I understand. But this might be important. By the way, I don't know your name. I didn't look inside your case."

"I'm Ivy Morton."

"Nice to meet you, Ivy."

"So, where should we meet?"

"There's a sandwich shop just up Western Avenue. Let's meet there; I'm parked in front of it."

"So am I! It was the only spot I could find. Shall we walk together?"

"Great!"

Ivy had never had an experience like this in her entire life. She was going to get coffee with a woman she had met only a few minutes before, but there was something about her; she felt perfectly safe being with this stranger. Veronica was very eager to talk, and Ivy was ready to hear what she had to say. And besides, Ivy was here to learn all she could about the Buster Keaton/Muskegon connection. Maybe this Veronica was the person to talk to, as the old woman had suggested.

≈

As the two walked down Western Avenue, Ivy told Veronica why she was at the film festival and a little bit about her book idea. Veronica was thrilled to have met the author of Ruby and Sal. She said she had been meaning to read the book, as she had heard about it from some friends.

"Why, I'm a little star-struck. And by the way," she said. "Call me Ronnie. Everyone does."

"Okay, Ronnie. I'd be happy to. Sorry, I don't have a nickname to offer," laughed Ivy. "And please, I'm nowhere near to being a star. It's only my first –

Ivy stopped dead in her tracks. Ronnie not realizing at first that Ivy was not moving with her had continued on a few steps. When she turned to see what the problem was, she was surprised to see Ivy's face had gone completely white. She looked like a deer in the headlights – wanting so badly to run but afraid to make a move.

"What's the problem?" When Ivy didn't answer, she tried again. "Ivy? Can I help you with anything? Are you okay?"

"Uh, yes, I – uh --" Ivy was having trouble forming a sentence, because she was looking across the street at a man and woman getting into a car -- a red sports car; they had just finished putting the top down. The man was wearing a homburg hat tipped down low over his forehead. He had on a double-breasted pinstriped suit, true to the era of the film festival. He was so handsome, it made Ivy's heart melt. Fox – Fox Marzetti -- the man who continued to haunt her dreams. The woman he was with was laughing at something; she was beautiful, of course, and why wouldn't she be? She was dressed in a flapper outfit from the 1920s, fringe, feathers, and all. Could she be one of Fox's many sisters? But no, no brother would lean in for a kiss with his arm around the woman's waist the way he had. Once she was sitting in the car and he had closed the passenger door, he walked around to the driver's side. As Ivy raised her hand to her mouth to stifle the cry she knew was close to escaping, he caught the movement and glanced up. He stood as still as the Buster Keaton monument for a moment and then slowly raised his hand for a sober wave and slight nod. Fox seemed so sad. They each stared across the street, standing perfectly still, wondering what to do next, until Ivy was able to break the connection. When Ronnie asked once again if she was all right, she was able to force her feet to proceed toward the sandwich shop.

"We're here, come inside and sit down," said Ronnie, sympathetically. "Are you okay now?"

"Yes, I'm fine. I was just in shock." The pallor Ronnie had first seen was disappearing as Ivy's normal color began to return.

"An ex? I've been there. Believe me, it's tough to see him with another woman, isn't it?"

"Yes, yes, it was. I was surprised by my reaction. I guess -- I mean I figured he must have moved on. But I was the one who called it off." Ivy grimaced at her childishness. "It was silly to think he would still be waiting for me. It's been over a year since our last disastrous conversation."

"Can I get you two anything?" Ivy was jarred out of her thoughts when the waitress approached the table. After having placed orders for two coffees, Ronnie reached her hand across the table and touched her hand lightly.

"I'd like to say it will get better, but I know that doesn't always happen. But if you chose to break up, it must have been for a good reason."

"That's the thing. I still question my decision on a daily basis. But it's too late now. Maybe someday I'll have a conversation with him, but now that I've seen him with her, I think it will be a while." Ivy sighed, then looked around the room. "Let's change the subject. This is a nice place."

"One of my favorite haunts. Good coffee, and that's all that's important to me." They paused a moment as the waitress filled the cups that were already on the table.

"Cream?"

When they each answered, no, she replied, "Sugar's on the table. Wave if you need anything."

"Thank you." Then turning back to Ivy, Ronnie said softly, "Now, about Gina."

"Yes, who is she, and why did she tell me to contact you?" Glad for the change in subject, Ivy was eager to learn about the mysterious woman she had met in the theater.

"I hope you don't think I'm weird, but there's something about her that has been bothering me all year, since last year's film festival. You see, I don't come to these things on a regular basis. Last year was my first time. I was alone, just like you, and Gina sat next to me. She asked some questions that seemed harmless. We chatted about my fascination with Buster Keaton, because my great-great-grandfather knew him. You see, my great-great-grandfather was named Max Woods, and he was in vaudeville. His father before him, was a man named Edward Woods, and he and his wife, my three times great-grandparents were in the circus."

"Wow, this is fascinating. Mind if I take notes?"

"Of course, not. Go ahead. Maybe you'll give me credit in your next book," chuckled Ronnie. "Well, anyway, when Gina found out about my family tree and the connection to Buster Keaton, she touched my hand.

46

Now, don't think I'm weird, but her touch was so warm. It was like I was being infused with something. The feeling went right through me. It was so bizarre. When I asked her name, she said just call me Gina."

Ivy's eyes widened with shock. "No, I don't think you're weird, not at all, because it happened to me, too, but she wouldn't tell me her name. What does it mean?"

"All I know is that she stressed I should come back to the theater at the same time next year, and look for a young woman my age. She said she would be carrying a tablet and pen, and that she would be alone. And then she left before the movie started. What she said bothered me all year long, and each time I did more family research, I felt more and more strongly that I needed to do as she suggested. So I actually came tonight to look for you, I guess."

"That's so bizarre. Last year at this time, I was just in the early stages of publishing Ruby and Sal. I had no idea that I would want to write another book. I never planned anything about Buster Keaton or the film festival. How could she know that?"

"I'm not sure, but she sure does look like a fortune teller or something. I asked around about her, and no one seems to know her. No one at the showing even saw her there but me. She came out of nowhere and disappeared immediately after."

Ivy was quiet a moment as she tried to digest everything that Ronnie had said. How could this old woman know about her life and what she was planning to write before she did? "So, if she is not a fake, and that's a big if, why did she want us to meet? What kind of information do you have that I might need? And why would she care?"

"I'm not sure about anything, but would you be interested in looking at my research about Bluffton and The Actor's Colony? My family was a part of it in the 1900s."

"Of course, I'll take all the help I can get. Any little thing can inspire me into a new story. But you know, Ruby and Sal was based on fact and then I embellished a little, but it's basically true. My great-grandparents really were part of a bootlegging operation and they really did know Al Capone. This book will be all fiction. I don't have a connection to Buster Keaton, at all."

"Well, maybe knowing some of the details I have on my family will help with your story. I have letters, pictures, and even a journal my grandmother kept. And I have been an avid collector of Buster Keaton memorabilia for years. I have copies of newspaper articles, and old postcards of the Muskegon area."

"Sounds fascinating. When can we meet again? I really need to get home. Someone is waiting for me."

Ronnie bit her lip, thinking about her schedule for the week. "I'm pretty busy all week long. Where do you live?"

"I'm from Whitehall. It's just a twenty-minute drive."

"Oh, wonderful. I thought you were from out of town. Do you have time tomorrow? I'll come to you. Well, only if you have a good coffee shop there," she laughed.

Ivy thought a moment. Could she trust this nice young woman? She had only known her for a few minutes, but she knew in her heart that this meeting was meant to be. So without hesitation she said, "That would be perfect. There's a good diner on the main street. You can't miss it. Lunch? They make great burgers."

"I'll be there, Ivy. Noon?"

"Sounds good. And thanks for coming to me. It helps a lot with – well, it helps a lot. See you there. It was so nice getting to know you, but I really have to run."

"Yes, me too. My husband will wonder where I am. I'm surprised he hasn't texted to check up on me. He's at home with the kids, but I guess no news is good news."

"Bye, Ronnie. Tomorrow, then. I'm anxious to see what you have to show me."

Chapter Three

When Ivy pulled into her parking lot at almost 10:30 in the evening, she realized that she had been completely unaware of the drive home. It had apparently been one of those dangerous drives where she was so deep in thought that she had been driving by rote, with no recollection of having driven at all. She was shaken to think that her thoughts of Fox were so all encompassing in such a way as to take over her entire being. She must be more careful. She had responsibilities, now. Someone needed her.

While sitting in her car for a few moments to compose herself, she wondered who the woman was who had been with him. Had he met her in Bay City? Was she a co-worker? Had he taken her to the cottage in Wabaningo? Had they slept together in Ruby and

Sal's bedroom? Had they danced on the dock under the moonlight? Her brain was tortured with unanswered questions. Realizing she would never know the answers, and forcing herself to believe that she didn't care anyway, she finally decided to go inside to someone who had probably missed her today.

Ivy fumbled with the doorknob while trying to turn the key, which caused a jiggling sound. Nancy was alerted that Ivy was home, so she was waiting at the door to greet her.

"Hey, you're back," she said in a whisper.

"Hi, how's S –

"Shhh. He's sleeping."

"Great. I wish I could have said goodnight, but I'm exhausted. I'll just peek in." Ivy removed her coat, so she didn't bring any cool air into the bedroom with her, and then she tiptoed across the hardwood floor. The nightlight cast a glow on his angelic face. She reached out and caressed the downy softness covering his perfectly round head with hair that, although light in color now, was sure to turn darker later. He made little sucking movements with his pink lips, probably dreaming about his next meal. Dimples flashed in his soft plump cheeks; inhaling deeply she bent down to kiss him. Oh, the sweet baby smell! She wondered if she would ever get used to having this incredible little person in her life. Ivy had no idea that whenever she thought of him or talked about him, her face lit up with such joy that it was contagious to anyone around her. But just as quickly as the joy in seeing his darling face had come to her, so had the pain. Because tonight the one person she had tried to erase from memory had resurfaced, and she was reminded that she may have made a terrible mistake.

Nancy was waiting with a hot cup of herbal tea steeping in Ivy's favorite blue willow cup. Her dear friend knew her so well, that she even knew her nighttime rituals. "So, how was he?" asked Ivy.

"A perfect angel, as usual. You sure do have it easy. I've never seen such a contented and happy baby. My sister's kids cried a lot when they were small."

"It's most likely because I'm with him all day long, and he never has a chance to cry. I read once that babies need to be left alone to cry it out, sometimes, but I don't believe in that. They cry for a reason – hunger, discomfort, or pain. Would you prefer a life of tears or no tears, if there was someone who could satisfy all of your needs?"

"Well, whatever you're doing is working so far. So tell me, how was it? Did you learn a lot for your next book?" Nancy had become Ivy's biggest fan, and most important of all, she had been there every step of the way through Ivy's pregnancy. She had even been her birthing coach, and now she retained the coveted title of Godmother, which she took very seriously.

"Oh, Nance, there's so much to tell you. But I'm afraid you're going to think I've gone off my rocker."

"What are you talking about? Weren't you just going to a Buster Keaton film? What could go wrong?"

Ivy went through the whole tale of the mysterious gypsy woman named Gina, and the accidental meeting with Veronica. She did not leave a thing out, which was the norm during their girl-talk sessions. When she described Gina and what she had said, Nancy was fascinated. When she came to the part about Fox, Nancy was caring and sympathetic. When she discussed her meeting with Veronica at the sandwich shop, she was riveted, asking pertinent questions along the way. Once she had the whole picture, she began to intersperse comments and speculations of her own.

"Are you sure this person named Veronica isn't part of a scam? Maybe she was planted there to follow up after this Gina left you."

"I have to admit to thinking that myself at first, but no, once you meet Ronnie, you'll see that she's genuine."

"Ronnie?"

"Oh, yes. Sorry, she asked me to call her that. And it fits her better than Veronica. She's so sweet, really. You'll love her."

"I will? How will I meet her?"

"Well, that all depends on if I see her more than twice."

"Twice?"

"I've set up a meeting time at the diner tomorrow afternoon. Can you watch him for me again for an hour or so?"

"Of course, but are you sure meeting her again is wise?" Nancy, always the mother hen, was worried that Ivy would be taken in by a stranger and fall for a con.

"She's genuine, I'm sure of it." Nancy raised her eyebrows, but Ivy continued on. "Really. She has something to show me about Buster Keaton. She's an avid Keaton collector. I might be able to pick up some facts that I can't find anywhere else. But just to be sure, I chose the diner as our meeting spot, you know, a public place."

"Okay, then. As long as you're careful. What time do you need me?"

"We said noon. So 11:30? Just so we can get the little guy settled, before I take off again. After that meeting I hope to do my research from home on the Internet and through email and books. I'm sorry to put you out like this."

"Stop, will you? You know I love him to pieces. I'd do anything for the little slugger. Besides, Matt is crazy about him, too. It's been giving him ideas. I think he might be ready to start our family." Nancy's face was glowing with anticipation.

"That's wonderful. Our children could grow up together and be friends. Wouldn't that be great? What would I ever have done without you, Nancy?" Ivy's eyes threatened to well with tears.

"We've been through that already. No more talk of it. I'm here for you. Loyal to the end." She laughed, but then a frown crossed her brow. "Now, what are you going to do about Fox?"

"What do you mean?"

"You know what I mean. Are you going to call him, text him? He knows you saw him, right?"

"We've been over this already. It looks like he's with someone now. I'm out of the picture. It's too late for me. It was pretty obvious. You should have seen them together, driving off in that little car he named Ruby."

Nancy detected a hint of jealousy crossing Ivy's face. "But, he's –

"No, stop. I'm not going there. I'm done. A lot has happened since I last saw him, and now he's just a memory, a summer fling that I'm hoping will soon fade away. Someday, I won't even remember his name."

"Well, I doubt that! He was a big part of your life, but I'll respect your wishes. No more talk of Fox – unless you want to that is."

"Thank you. Now, you'd better get home and get some rest. You have a big day of babysitting again tomorrow." Ivy walked Nancy to the door, and as the two hugged goodbye, Ivy thanked God for her wonderful neighbor and friend.

Even though Ivy lived close to the diner -- it was only a matter of minutes from her apartment -- she was the last to arrive. She spotted Ronnie at a round corner

58

table by the window, busily pulling documents out of a large divided folder. Each division was labeled with tabs for easy reading. Looking over her new friend's shoulder, Ivy could see that her handwriting was neat and very legible.

"Hi, sorry I'm late. I had a little crisis at home."

"Oh hi, Ivy. No, I was a little early, actually. I hope your crisis wasn't anything too bad. We can postpone if you need to."

"Oh no, nothing like that. My son created a major diaper mess at the last minute, and I had to change his entire outfit."

"I've been there, believe me. It always has to happen at the worst time, right?"

Ivy pulled out a chair and hung her purse strap over the back, while removing her coat. She asked, "So, you have children?"

Ronnie smiled the way mother's do when talking about their offspring. "Yes, I have two little ones."

"Boys? Girls?"

"One of each. Cindy is 5 now and Timmy is 3. And yours?"

"I have a seven-month-old boy," said Ivy proudly. "Would you like to see a picture? Oh, never mind, that's what all parents do, and I hate it."

"Of course, don't be silly. I love baby pictures."

Ivy reached behind her into the bag hanging over the chair. She pulled out her phone and flipped through a few recent shots. As the two women bent their heads together, they appeared to be longtime friends or relatives to others who might be looking on. They oohed and aahed about their children for a little while until Ivy said, "I guess we'd better get started, here. I don't want to keep you all day, and I was away from my little guy most of yesterday."

"Of course. My kids are with my mom today, and my husband's at his buddy's house watching the Lions play, so I'm free, but just call it quits when you need to."

"Do you want something to drink? Pop? Coffee? It's on me – a write-off, you know," laughed Ivy.

"I'm a coffee addict, so a cup sounds nice. Thanks."

Ivy waved to the server and put two fingers in the air. In no time at all, the mugs which had been left on the table upside down were turned over and being filled to the brim. "Now, what have you got?"

"First, I have these postcards of Muskegon. If you've never seen any of these, you might find them interesting. This one is Pere Marquette Park at Lake Michigan in 1910. It was called Lake Michigan Park then. You can see the performance house which was right down on the beach in the pavilion. This is where all of the vaudevillians came to perform in the early 1900s. Wasn't it wonderful? They kept enlarging it, until the theater was able to hold over 1200 people. There was a restaurant and bowling alley in the lower level. Look at this one. By 1916 there was a figure-eight roller coaster on the beach, a Ferris wheel, a skating rink, and a miniature passenger train. It's been said that over 4000 people came each year for the Fourth of

July celebration alone. The park was known as the 'Coney Island of the West'."

Ivy studied each postcard she was handed, taking notes of small details for future reference. "I took the walking tour of Bluffton yesterday afternoon, before I went to the screening. I was amazed at all of the cottages that had belonged to vaudevillians."

"The story goes that the Keatons, along with others, came to Muskegon a few times to perform and Joe Keaton, Buster's father, fell in love with the area, so in 1907 he built a cottage right at the base of Pigeon Hill on Muskegon Lake. Funny, but in all of the old accounts, Buster always calls it Lake Muskegon. Anyway, by 1908 the cottage was finished and the Keatons returned here every summer after that until 1917 when Buster left the family act. That's when the act fell apart and the Keatons stayed behind while their other two children went to school. But let me back up. Before that, in 1908, Joe began convincing other friends of his to come to Muskegon also, so within a short period of time over 200 vaudevillians were summering here. You see, without air conditioning the city theaters were extremely hot, so people didn't attend the shows during the summer months. With attendance down most vaudevillians took the summers off preferring to use the time perfecting their acts. Spending time in Muskegon at the beach was a perfect solution. They would try out new acts on each other and then do a performance for the locals. The streetcars would take the Muskegon residents from the city to the beach for only five cents. While there they could attend a vaudeville show. Once the dancehall was added, it was a swinging place. How I would have loved to have seen it." Ronnie's face was lit up like a Christmas tree as she talked about her hobby and the facts about Muskegon she knew so well.

"The Keatons and others formed a club called The Actor's Colony. They actually built a clubhouse they named Rafters and Cobwebs."

"How old was Buster during all of this? He was born in 1895, wasn't he?"

"Yes, so I guess he was about 12 when they first came here. He couldn't wait for each summer to come around so he could come back to Muskegon and play with his friends. He loved a good game of baseball, and to this day a ballgame is played at the same park during the film festival week in his honor. The kids would run up and down Pigeon Hill, and tear up the neighborhood. He was always finding ways to prank people one way or another. That's where my great-great-grandfather comes in."

"What do you mean?" asked Ivy, now more curious than ever.

"Well, I have more pictures and letters, etc. The table is getting rather crowded. Is there someplace else we can go? A library, maybe?"

Ivy bit her lip wondering if she was right to do what she was about to suggest. But looking at the pleasant rounded face of her companion, she knew there was nothing to fear. Ronnie was on the up and up, she was positive of that. She already felt a kinship with her new friend. "We can always go to my place.

My friend has been babysitting a lot lately, anyway. I should give her a break. It's only a few blocks away."

"Okay, that sounds good, if you're sure I'm not going to impose."

"Not at all, I can't wait to hear what you have to say next. I'll help you pack up, and you can follow me over."

Chapter Four

The text read, *Warning! Bringing company. Be there in a few.*

Ivy thought it was only fair that she let Nancy know she was bringing Ronnie. When she opened the door, Nancy raised her eyebrows, making a face behind Ronnie's back. Ivy mouthed, 'It's really okay,' and smiled at her, reassuringly. But there was no need for worry on Nancy's part, because as soon as she was introduced to Ronnie, she felt her warmth and friendliness, the same as Ivy had.

The three women began to coo and smile at the infant sitting in the baby carrier.

"He's adorable," said Ronnie. "And what a beautiful complexion. Hi, handsome," she said to the baby. Ivy's son smiled flirtatiously and then ducked his head in a coy way. "Oh boy, watch out. He's already figured out how to work the ladies."

"Ivy, I have an idea," interjected Nancy. "I was just about ready to feed him, and then he'll probably nap. How about if I take him to my place, and then you two can get down to business without interruptions."

"Oh Nancy, that would be perfect. Are you sure you don't mind? I'll owe you big time."

"Already done. No problem. Besides, Matt is home and I'd like to give him a taste of having a baby in the house, know what I mean? Come on, slugger, come to Aunt Nancy."

Once she was loaded up with the essentials, Nancy carried the baby and carrier down the hall to the next apartment, while Ivy and Ronnie began to remove photos and postcards once again from the folder, spreading them all over the table.

"So, where should we start?" asked Ivy. "You take the lead."

"As I was saying at the diner, I have a personal interest in Buster Keaton, because my great-great-grandfather knew him well. Do you have a piece of paper? I'll jot down names so you don't lose track."

"Here, I can rip a piece out of my notepad."

"Okay, it goes like this. My three times great-grandfather was Edward Woods. He was a circus performer for Barnum and Bailey."

"Really? That's so cool. What time period are you talking about?"

"Back in the 1890s. He and his wife, my three times great-grandmother, were in the area on tour -- Muskegon, as well as other cities in Western Michigan, was on the Barnum and Bailey route. The circus was in Muskegon in August of 1890 and again in 1892. I actually found the circus schedule on line to verify my facts. Edward and his wife had been talking about leaving the circus and this town was exactly what they were looking for. For the first few months they lived in an apartment in the city, but Edward had decided he wanted to live closer to Lake Michigan, so they moved to Bluffton, and that's where Max Woods, my two times great-grandfather, was born -- in 1895, the same year as

Buster. By the time Max was twelve, the Keatons and others began coming to Muskegon Lake. Max and Buster became good friends along with several other kids in the area, so I've grown up with stories about Buster all of my life; hence, the fascination."

"That is truly amazing," commented Ivy, as she was looking over more pictures.

"Yes, I think I have some pictures that no one else has. They were in boxes of photos that were passed down, and when I began to sort through them, I found some of various people who were members of The Actor's Colony. Look, here's one of Mush Rawls with Max. And this one is a picture of a group of them at a party – looks like a wedding – the bride and groom are in the center. It says on the back that it's August 15th of 1913; unfortunately the people aren't named, but I've been able to identify some of them."

Ivy brought the photo up close to her face, then she jumped up and went to her kitchen junk drawer. As Ronnie looked on in puzzlement, she rummaged around until she found what she was looking for – a magnifying glass.

"Who is this? Ronnie, do you know who this young girl is? The one right here?" Ronnie could see that Ivy was shaken. She leaned in closer to see what Ivy was pointing at. But before she had a chance, Ivy pulled back the photo once more and studied it with the glass in hand. Then she shoved it back at Ronnie.

"Let me see. Why, that's Max's first wife. I can't recall her name, right now. I'm the offspring of wife number two. What's wrong? You look like you've seen a ghost."

Ivy was quiet a moment as she tried to pull her thoughts together. "Remember when we thought Gina was strange for wanting us to get together?"

"Yes, of course. It's was quite weird."

"Well, I might know the reason why."

"Hurry, don't leave me in suspense. What have you discovered?"

"I'm not for sure. It's all very strange and doesn't make sense, yet. But that pretty young woman, or girl really, is wearing a very interesting necklace. Did you notice it?"

"Let me look again. I've never paid much attention to it. It is pretty, but without color it's impossible to say what it really looked like."

"I'm looking at the formation and design of the stones. When I look through the magnifier, I can see there are five large stones with smaller ones around each of the big ones. They seem to have a sparkle, even though it's a black and white photo. It's almost jumping off the paper. Or is it just my imagination?"

"I'm not sure. Maybe. I never noticed that before. Her dress sure is pretty. I loved those styles didn't you? The high waist, the way the soft fabric draped their bodies, and the large hats – to die for."

"It can't be," said Ivy to herself.

"What is it that has gotten you so excited?"

"My great-grandmother described a necklace she used to have. I've never actually seen it, except in one photo that I have of her. It had five large rubies and each one was surrounded by diamonds. She left it to me, but after she died we were unable to find it."

"Are you talking about THE ruby necklace in Ruby and Sal? I thought that was all fiction. I read the back cover blurb last night, and I remember that it mentioned a mysterious necklace."

"Believe it or not, most of that story was the truth. I had to add embellishments to make it readable fiction for the public, but the necklace did exist at one time. And now, here is a girl wearing a necklace like it in a photo that you own, and you say it was your two times great-grandfather's first wife. Here, let me get the photo of Ruby. Look, what do you think? Is it the same one or one like it?"

"Well, I just got chills. I started reading your book last night, but I haven't gotten to anything about a necklace yet, but if it is the same necklace, how did it get to your great-grandmother? Are we related in some way?"

"Let's take a look at your family tree again. No, I don't see the connection. I've never heard of these people." Ivy bit her lip in thought.

Suddenly, Ronnie said, "Oh my! This is very strange, amazing, actually. It's all coming together now. I'm not sure how your great-grandfather got that necklace, but I do have a story to tell you that has been passed down through the generations, and I have a journal to back it up. How much time do we have?" Ronnie was so excited she was almost coming unglued.

"Let me go down the hall and get little Sal, and then I can put him to bed before we start talking."

"Sal? Like the book?"

"Yes, I named him after my great-grandfather," said Ivy beaming. "His full name is Salvatore, but we call him Bud or Buddy. I try calling him Sal every now and then, so he'll know his true name, but he just doesn't seem like a Sal, yet. I'm hoping he'll grow into it. I was planning to have a girl, so I could name her Ruby, but little Sal came out instead," laughed Ivy.

"How sweet. Well, you get Buddy, and I'll call my mother. I'm sure she can handle the kids another few hours. This is going to be too good for you to miss. Have I got a story for you!"

Intrigued, Ivy hurried next door to collect her little bundle who was already nodding his head and ready for a nap. Once he was settled in his crib, she tiptoed out, leaving the door open a crack in case he woke up, and the two settled on the couch with a glass of Moscato, tablets and pens, pictures spread out all around them, and pillows stacked behind their backs. Ivy started the fire to set the perfect ambience for storytelling. As Ronnie recounted her story, Ivy took notes; sometimes she gasped with surprise and sometimes she cried with either sympathy or amazement, but she never interrupted, because she was already forming her next novel in her mind. And most important of all was the fact that this story was so incredible she could hardly believe it was true, and because of a mystical woman with clairvoyant powers, it had been plopped right into her lap.

Maisy and Max, 1890–1917

Chapter Five

Edward walked back to the circus grounds with the necklace on the inside pocket of his jacket. It vibrated with each step and seemed as if it were warming his heart. He had a new outlook, an excitement that had not been there before. He was about to get everything he had ever dreamed of and more; he just knew it. He was about to propose to the woman of his dreams. She didn't know it yet, of course; she didn't even know she was the woman he dreamt of every night before falling asleep with the sound of lions roaring and elephants trumpeting in the background. But he had been in love with her since she first joined the circus with her family two years ago. She was a part of the exotic cat show. Maureen would quite often go into the cage with a whip, keeping the cats on their individual stands, while her father performed some death defying act, like placing his head inside the mouth of a Bengal tiger. Maureen's bravery and concentration kept her father safe; she literally held her father's life in her hands, and that is why Edward admired her so. Well, that and the fact that she wore the skimpiest costume of all of the women in the circus, and her plump white cleavage reminded him of a soft pillow he would love to lay his head on. Edward knew how Maureen loved flashy clothes and jewelry, so he decided to give her the necklace this very afternoon. He was sure she would be so enraptured with it, that she would agree to go out with him, and then he could move things along from there. With the magic the rubies would bring -- and he knew without a doubt that they were real -- he was convinced she would be his in no time.

Even though it was still raining, more of a drizzle, really, he whistled as he walked, taking his time as he planned how he would approach the love of his life. As soon as he was on the grounds, he headed straight to Maureen's tent. He had already planned out the dialogue he would use to convince her of his worth. Because there were no doors, most of the tents had some type of bell to ring before entering, but in his eagerness, he pulled back the flap as he did at his own tent, neglecting to warn the occupant of his presence. What he saw totally devastated him. Maureen was sitting on her table with her bloomers pulled down and her legs in the air. Standing in front of her was the tight rope walker, Antonio; his pants in a heap around his ankles. His thrusting movement was something Edward had never witnessed before, because even though he had been around animals all of his life, and in fact had taken part in this very act himself on a few occasions, he had never seen human love-making performed. For a moment he was riveted, but then he quickly realized that he was watching a very private act. Whether love or pure sex, he should not be a voyeur; it was just wrong.

Edward walked slowly back toward his own tent. The grounds had become a muddy mess as the rain had started to fall at a heavier rate. He was wet and chilled as he passed the ticket booth. His head hung in utter desolation. This was not the way he had planned his day. Nothing had gone right from the very beginning. He decided then and there he was through with the circus. His juggling act would have to be filled by someone else once they reached the States and began the winter hiatus. In his misery, he didn't notice, at first, as a young woman in the booth called out to him, but on her second call, he heard his name and looked up. It was Clara.

"Hey, Edward, you look cold. Want to come inside and get dried off a bit? I have some hot tea ready."

His head, still foggy from the obscene vision he had recently witnessed, Edward wasn't quite sure what she was saying to him. He swayed a moment like a drunken man, and suddenly the warmth at his chest ran through his whole body. He moved forward with steps that seemed out of his control, and then he felt a strong vibration as he neared Clara. 'Why haven't I noticed before?' he wondered. Clara, his friend, had always been there for him. She listened to his troubles and had a kind mothering way about her, even though she wasn't much over nineteen or twenty. He walked silently to her; she took his hand and led him to her tent, which was just around the corner from the big tent. She knew instinctively something was seriously wrong with Edward, and since she had been in love with him since the day she first set eyes on him, she wanted nothing more than to fix his hurt and soothe his pain.

Clara removed Edward's wet coat and sat him next to a small wood burning tubular firepot that all circus performers carried to help with those cold damp days. It was dangerous to have fire of any kind around the tents and animals, but there was no other way to keep warm on the road. She wrapped him up in a blanket, and served him hot chamomile tea. He placed his hands around the cup, soaking up its heat, and when he looked at Clara gratefully, he couldn't believe how beautiful she was. The flickering light cast shadows on her face, enhancing her innocent sensuality; she was radiant with happiness. How had he missed it? She was of slight build, with almost white blonde hair piled on top of her head. The reflection of the fire caused her locks to emit a halo-like light. Her light blue dress formed to her contours nicely, coming up to her neck with a ruffle at the top. He could tell that her shape was trim and quite pleasant, very pleasant, indeed, even though she was nowhere near as well-endowed as Maureen. And most striking were her blue eyes which were full of kindness and love. The total package was perfect for a man in need of a wife and confidant. He could see in an instant that she would make a great life partner and mother someday, which is really all he had dreamed of. Maureen had been a pipe dream. She was never meant for him, he could see that now. How had he missed what had been right in front of him all this time? The warmth at his chest grew stronger. He had an overwhelming urge to kiss her, but he knew it was too soon.

The two sat in the secluded coziness of the tent as Edward told Clara that he was fine, he had just been having a bad day. He was embarrassed that she had seen him like this. He left out the experience with the gypsy and the necklace he was carrying in his breast pocket, and he never once mentioned the incident with Maureen and Antonio, but he did tell her his doubts about remaining in the circus life. She expressed that she had the same misgivings about the circus. She had never felt as though she fit in. It was her parents who had wanted to travel the world with the circus, and even though they had no performing talents, they were good at their jobs, which was the managing aspects of it all. Her mother booked new acts and set the performing order, while her father kept them harmoniously working together. But Clara was a lover of books and a voracious reader; she said she had had enough traveling experience to last a lifetime. She would rather live her life through the printed word. There were other parts of life that she wanted to experience, like being a mother. She also expressed her desire to live in a real house with a yard; she wanted to take care of a husband and her many children.

As she talked, Edward fell more in love with her with each passing moment. The sound of her voice was like music to his ears. All the dreams she mentioned for her future were the same as he had thought about for himself. Edward and Clara talked way into the night, and with the necklace getting hotter against his shirt, and his attraction growing stronger, Edward did not hesitate a moment when she asked him to stay the night. He simply smiled with joy and pulled her to him. Clara confessed to being a virgin. In the circus world of free sexuality, that was truly something rare. He had found his own gem in a world of flashing lights and illusions.

Edward was also pleasantly surprised that even with Clara's inexperience she was a wonderful lover. From that night on, the two were never apart, and soon Edward presented her with the ruby necklace as a birthday gift. After that their nights together seemed enhanced beyond his wildest dreams. Clara was surprised with herself. She had never felt so free. Whenever she wore the necklace and she and Edward were together, she felt like she was flying in another universe. And every time their two bodies merged into one, they became more and more bonded. Soon, Edward moved his things into her tent, and they set up a household without the benefits of marriage, and no one thought one thing about it. That was circus life in the 1890s.

In the evenings when they were alone, Edward would bring out the schedule as they tried to decide what they would do with their lives next. Edward would lay out a map, and as they looked at what was ahead for them, they both agreed that the last time they were in Western Michigan they had loved it there. As Clara's finger trailed down the projected cities they would be stopping at, they were thrilled to see that Muskegon was on the list for August 21st.

"Isn't that the place that is so close to Lake Michigan?" Clara asked.

"Yes, look here. It's the one with that huge beach area and the channel that runs into that large lake. Lake Muskegon, isn't it?"

"Oh, yes. I loved it there. We had some time off the last time we passed through, so I was able to go to the beach for a few minutes. I would love to live in an area like that."

Edward laughed at her phrasing. "Why an area *like* that? Why not *that* area? What do you say we get off the circus train in Muskegon and never look back?"

"Really? What are you saying?"

"Marry me, Clara. I love you more than life itself. We can be happy there. I'll build you a house with a picket fence, just the way you always dreamed. And someday we can add children to the picture." Edward held his breath. They had never discussed marriage. Each had been afraid to jinx their relationship with the mention of it.

Clara squealed and threw herself at Edward. She had been waiting for him to propose since the day she first met him. "Yes, yes! I'll marry you, Edward Woods. We'll live in Muskegon Michigan and have many, many children. I'll be the best wife you could ever imagine."

"Oh, Clara, you have made me the happiest man ever. I'm sorry I don't have a ring for you. I should have planned ahead."

"But Edward, we have the necklace," she grinned flirtatiously, as she pushed him back on their cot. "Who needs a ring?"

$$\approx$$

The trip across the Atlantic seemed to take forever, but Edward and Clara were excited to leave dreary London behind. They spent the winter hiatus planning and dreaming about their new home, but they were extremely secretive about their life-changing decision. They needed the circus to continue paying them until they were ready to leave and also it was good for free transportation to the Midwest.

The circus began to move again in April, zigzagging its way across New York, Pennsylvania, Indiana, Illinois, Ohio, and then finally, in August, they headed across the state border into Michigan. The young couple was so excited they could hardly contain themselves, but they waited until the night before the

Muskegon performance, which was to be held on the afternoon of August 1st. Clara decided it was best if she approached her father alone so she could explain what they had in mind, but Edward wanted to be by her side. It was surprisingly easy. Clara's father said the family had always known she wasn't happy and never expected her to stay this long. There were many young girls biting at the bit to sell tickets in the booth just to be a part of the circus. The family gave them their blessing and said she would be missed, but every year in August when the circus was in Michigan, they could see each other again.

Edward went straight to the ringmaster after that, because telling Clara's father and mother took care of finding their replacements, since they were the overall managers. But telling the ringmaster was almost humiliating. He laughed and said good riddance; he said Edward had never been a good juggler, anyway. Others could do many more tricks than he; it would be easy to replace him, he said. It was quite bruising to

Edward's ego to hear this, but the putdown had made his life changing decision so much easier.

After the Friday afternoon performance, the happy couple packed up their personal items in the tent, which belonged to the circus. They gave away many things that they could not carry and took only what was necessary to survive. They collected their final pay, and waved as the train took their family and friends away. Everything they had ever known was chugging down the rails, leaving nothing but a smoke trail behind. The two lovers were nervous but excited about their new life.

The first thing they did was to ask a stranger about a boarding house. He told them there were several about a mile away, in the center of the residential district. It was a hot miserable day, but the two didn't mind the trek in the least. Laughing like children, they could hardly wait to see where their new life would take them.

Things were difficult at first. Neither one had any experience outside of the circus, but at least Clara had learned how to handle money and make change. She had always been good with customers, so she applied for a position at the local grocery market, and she was hired instantly. Edward obtained a job at Kitchen Coal and Ice Company. He was required to unload the trains when they arrived with coal and then load it onto a delivery wagon. He already knew how to handle horses and had been around trains all of his life. He was a good employee so he sometimes received bonuses, which the two stashed away for their dream home.

Less than a year later they were able to save enough for a move to Bluffton on Lake Muskegon. They would be renting a small cottage that wasn't even winterized, but they were thrilled to be near the water where they could take leisurely walks after work and fish off the docks for their supper, and most importantly, they could catch the trolley to town and their jobs for only three cents a trip.

One night when Edward had arrived home late, because the train delivery had been delayed, he found Clara standing in their kitchen wearing nothing but her chemise and the ruby necklace. The minute Edward laid eyes on her, he wanted her like he had at no other time.

"What's the occasion?" he asked, as he playfully ran his hands over her body.

Clara's eyes were soft and inviting. "I think it's time we try to make a baby. What do you think?"

Edward roared with laughter. "Haven't we already been doing that, over and over again? You're unquenchable, even though I have been doing my best to satisfy you."

Clara lowered her eyes, almost afraid to tell Edward what she had been doing. "Well, you see, I have been taking a certain herb that one of the girls at the circus told me about. I didn't think we were ready to have children, yet. I wanted to make sure we had a home and could feed a child. But now we are truly ready, don't you think?"

"I wondered why we had not seen any results of all of my hard work." He laughed, "But you were right to do so. Now we can follow our plan to the letter. It's

time to have a family. Let's get to it, girl!" And he lifted
up the love of his life and carried her to their bedroom.

Chapter Six

The year was 1894, four years after Edward and Clara had left the circus. Their love was strong, but they had not yet been able to conceive a child. It was not for lack of trying, the ruby necklace saw to that. But each month that came around told Clara that it was not to be. She tried hard to keep her spirits high at first, but soon it began to wear on her, especially when she saw other women with their brood, some of whom were popping one out every year. Edward worried about Clara, because he knew that a husband and children were all she had ever wanted. They continued to work and save until they were able to buy a larger house near the cottage they had been renting. It was warmer in the winter and cooler in the summer, and they were still near all of the wonderful neighbors they had grown so close to. It was perfect, except for the missing voices of children playing and the sound of running feet throughout the house.

Then one afternoon, late in September, Edward arrived home to the mouth-watering smell of a pot roast dinner, his favorite. Clara was at the stove in her long ruffled apron, looking like a magazine cover, with her hair upswept and the bustle at her back giving her backside a rounded and sensual look. But most noticeably was the fact that she was wearing the cherished necklace.

Edward moved in close and nuzzled her neck. "Did I forget an anniversary?"

With stirring spoon in hand, Clara turned to him, tears glistening in her eyes, and she simply said, "I'm going to have a baby."

Edward whooped and hollered not even afraid that the neighbors would hear him through the open windows. He picked up his lovely wife and twirled her about and then gingerly put her down. "Did I hurt you? I shouldn't have done that. I'm sorry."

Clara laughed at the tortured look on his face. "I'm okay, Edward. I'm not fragile. I won't break."

"Can we still – um." He pointed to the bedroom with his thumb.

"Yes, my love, we can – um." She laughed and imitated his thumb gesture.

"A baby! A baby! What will we name him?"

"Her, you mean?"

"Maybe one of each?"

"Now let's don't get ahead of ourselves. We have a ways to go."

"When do you think?" asked Edward, breathlessly.

"Probably about March of next year."

"Oh, such a long time. But that will give us time to prepare, won't it."

"Yes, Edward, but let's take one thing at a time. Right now the roast needs another half hour of cooking, so what do you say we celebrate?"

Edward kissed his lovely wife gently at first and then with excited passion as he began the task of untying her apron.

≈

The winter months dragged on for the couple who were so eager for their bundle of joy to arrive. Clara quit her job at the grocery store, because Edward had been made supervisor and the pay increase allowed them to live off of one income. Clara sewed quilts in pastel colors, knit both blue and pink baby sweaters and bonnets just to be prepared, and consulted with the neighbor ladies about other baby needs.

Edward boasted to his friends about becoming a father. They were eager to share the stories of the worst part of having children, from sleepless nights to runny noses and diarrhea, but Edward never let it bother him one bit; he was ready for the responsibility, no matter what hardships it might bring.

The night finally came when Clara leaned over her husband in bed and poked Edward awake out of a sound sleep. "It's time," she simply said.

He jumped up and pulled on his pants, then ran down the street to the midwife's house. He pounded on the door and begged her to come quickly. "Don't worry," she said. "The first one always takes a long time. There's no rush."

The midwife sat with Clara through the rest of the night and into the morning and late afternoon as she perspired, moaned, and rolled on the bed. Edward had taken the day off from work and was in misery listening to his wife's pain. He was encouraged to take a walk outside, where he sat on the end of the dock so he could pray for Clara's health and the safety of the child. When he returned he was rewarded with the sound of a baby crying. The midwife was holding his child – his child. He thought his chest would burst, until he saw the look on her face.

"I'm so sorry, Edward, but Clara didn't make it."

"What? What do you mean, she didn't make it? She's healthy; she's young; she was waiting for her baby to arrive. *We* were waiting. This can't be. I need to see her. I need to --"

"Yes, go ahead. I'll take care of the baby. Take all the time you need."

The sounds of Edward's sobbing was almost unbearable for the midwife to hear, but she had heard it before. It was not uncommon for women to die in childbirth. Most important now would be the health of the child. As soon as Edward came out, looking as pale as a ghost, she said, "I have to leave now, for a few moments, to find a woman who can nurse your child. He needs nourishment."

"He? It's a boy?" asked Edward through his tears. It was then that he held his son for the first time. As he gazed upon the infant's face, he saw his Clara's eyes, and Clara's nose. He fell in love with his son instantly, because it was all he had left of their dream.

When Mrs. Gordon arrived to nurse the baby, he went back to the bedroom; he kissed his wife goodbye one last time. He picked up the ruby necklace Clara had left on the nightstand. Since they were unable to use it the last few months, she had liked to keep it close by. As he held it in his hands, he thought of his love and how beautiful she had looked whenever she wore it. But it had lost its luster and was as cold as winter ice. In a white hot anger, he threw the ruby necklace across the room, vowing that it would never be worn by anyone ever again.

Chapter Seven

Throughout the next six months, Edward struggled with being a single father. He would work delivering coal and ice all day, whatever the season and weather, and then come home to take over the care of the baby from Mrs. Gordon. Alice Gordon had five children of her own, and when she had lost number six, after it had survived for only a few short days, she was more than happy to take over being the nursemaid to little Max; she cherished feeling the warmth of an infant in her arms to fill the void of her lost child at her breast. At the age of six weeks, Maxwell Jeremiah Woods was christened just the way his mother had planned, named after no one in particular, but with the name Edward and Clara had both agreed on for a boy's name, if they were so blessed. His hair and complexion were showing signs of following after his father's Romani roots, but he had the eyes of his mother. He was a beautiful child.

Since Alice had a full house, and it was difficult for her to come to him, Edward would drop Max off at her place in the morning and pick him up in the evening. Edward tried his best to be the father Clara would have wanted him to be. He whispered stories to Max about his mother, the circus, and the magic necklace as he rocked him, but of course the infant was too young to understand a word of it. After his rage had cooled, on the night he had thrown the necklace across the room, and once Clara's body had been removed from the bed they had shared, Edward had returned to pick up the rubies from the corner of the floor in hopes that he could feel Clara's warmth, but it was as lifeless as she was. He dropped it into the small box that Clara had always kept it in, and never looked at it again.

The women in the neighborhood realized they had two problems to solve, and they immediately began working on the solution. Edward needed someone to care for Max, and Lena Barnett needed a husband to provide for her and her two children. She had recently lost her husband due to an accident at his work where he had fallen off a ladder. She had been alone for almost the exact same time as Edward had. She was ten years older than Edward, but age was not important, because there was a greater need to fill than ego. The neighborhood women suggested to Edward that he should court Lena, and the sooner the better. Their joining together could be beneficial to them both. Although Edward and Lena were still in mourning, they agreed to see each other for a walk and tea. They shared stories of their loved ones, and talked about their children. Lena had a boy and a girl, ages 8 and 10. She was more than willing to care for little Max and cook and clean for Edward. There was no spark or sexual attraction of any kind, but they agreed to forgo the one-year mourning period and marry for companionship and financial reasons. Lena said she was not interested in the intimate side of marriage, and Edward said that was fine with him. He couldn't imagine being with anyone other than Clara. They were married within two weeks' time, and the two households were joined into one at Edward's cottage, because it was bigger.

Max thrived under Lena's care, and soon her children fell in love with the baby and felt as though the five of them had always been one family. They enjoyed having a father around the house again -- someone to play with and teach them things that only a man would know. All was well, until Edward began to feel the stirring that all men feel, but when he reached for Lena in their bed one night, she rejected him. Eventually, she did give in, submitting to her wifely duty with no emotion whatsoever. It was enough to satisfy Edward for a while, but he missed the wild abandonment he had shared with Clara. He longed for that kind of passion again, but he refused to offer the ruby necklace to Lena -- he wasn't sure it would work on her, anyway. She wasn't even aware of its existence; he had hidden it in a box of Clara's personal items when they were first married. After a time he visited the professional girls in a house he had heard of through the grapevine. He wasn't proud of himself, and he knew Clara wouldn't be, either, but he had no other place to go that would not get him into trouble. He was not about to start an affair with someone else's wife.

For the most part, Edward was happy with his arrangement. He liked to show the children some of his juggling moves as they laughed and clapped and squealed for more, but it was Max who showed real talent. From the time he was able to walk, he was always trying to throw things in the air and catch them. He consistently sported a bruise on his face or the top of his head from a tossed toy gone awry. Eventually, as he grew older, he developed an impressive ability for juggling. Edward was proud that his son was able to accomplish more than he had at his age.

In 1907 when Max was 12 years old, he met a boy named Buster. All the kids were talking about him and the vaudeville act he performed with his parents who traveled around the country with a troupe. From the time the Keatons first arrived in Bluffton, the kids were impressed with the boy who could fall without getting hurt, and who knew how to perform on stage in front of an audience doing his stone-faced comedy routine with his father. Like the Pied Piper had rats following him out of town, Buster had boys in Bluffton following him *around* the town; he had a personality that drew them in like a magnet. They eagerly awaited for him to arrive at his summer home each June, when they would organize a baseball game in the field, or chase each other up and down the huge dune called Pigeon Hill. When the boys weren't busy doing chores, they spent a lot of time swimming, fishing, and skipping rocks. Max was fascinated with Buster's vaudeville experiences; he was constantly asking questions about the acts and how they traveled and where they went. At the same time he began to inquire about Edward's experiences in the circus.

One day, when Max was fishing with his father, he asked, "Pa, will you tell me about the circus?"

"Max, I think I've told you all of my stories. You've heard them since you were a baby."

"I know, but I'd like to hear them again, now that I'm older. Mother won't let you talk about it to me in

104

her presence, but I want to know about my real mother and her past with you."

"I understand, son. I will tell you everything you want to know, but you have to promise not to let your mother, Lena, know what I say. It has to be our secret, okay? She gets upset when she thinks of my past life. I think she's afraid I'll corrupt her children and they'll want to run off. You don't, do you? Want to run off, I mean."

"Well, I might. I mean, I've thought about it. Not to get away from you, but because I really want adventure. Buster and his mom and dad and brother and sister travel all over the place."

"Yes, Max, but have you ever noticed how happy Buster is when he arrives in Bluffton? He has no stability. He calls this place his home, and he's only here for the summers. What kind of life is that for a boy?" Edward was starting to feel fear. He couldn't bear to lose Max. He fussed with his lure while trying to quiet his pounding heart.

"Aw, Pa, I wouldn't go for a long time. And I'll wait until I'm grown and take my wife with me."

"Oh, Max, you make me laugh, but you scare me, too. I don't want you to move away. You're all I have left of your mother."

"I know, that's why I'll wait to leave until I'm older. I want to juggle in front of people like Buster does. I want to make people laugh and clap for me. I want to be a star."

"I think you have some of your grandparents' wanderlust and love of the circus in you," he said as he cast out his line. "I'll tell you the good and bad of it. Then when you're older, you can make up your own mind. Maybe you'll see that circus life isn't all that it appears on the surface. That's why your mother and I left."

After that day, whenever Edward and Max were alone, whether it was repairing a roof, or working on the front porch, or driving into town for supplies, Edward told Max everything. He told him about the gypsy, the necklace she had given him, and how he had found

Clara and given the necklace to her instead of a ring. Of course, he left out the part about seeing the woman he thought he loved with another man, but he did describe his walk through the rain past the ticket booth and Clara, and how she had invited him into her tent to dry off. But he never told Max the power the necklace held for the two lovers. Mostly, he just wanted Max to know that he was loved, and what a wonderful person his real mother, Clara, was.

The talks only cemented the fact that Max wanted to travel. But in the summer of 1908, when Max turned thirteen, a new girl moved to Bluffton, and Max fell in love. Her name was Maisy Abernathy. The exact opposite of Max in coloring, she had white blonde hair and huge blue eyes. She was the only child of a seamstress. There was no father around so the mother and daughter took in as much sewing as they could and did laundry for the wealthy people who came to summer in their cottages and didn't want to be bothered with mundane chores. Max admired Maisy from afar for a while, afraid to make a move and show his hand. The problem was that another boy named Earl was interested in her, too, and he was not shy, at all. He followed Maisy around and tried to talk to her whenever he had a chance. Max couldn't tell if she was interested in Earl or not, so he stayed in the background, dreaming of her every night, and wondering if she would like going off to the circus with him.

One day he was walking along the street in front of his house, juggling balls as he went, the same as he always did, when he heard someone say, "Hey, you're pretty good."

Max looked up to see who was talking, and immediately dropped the balls. He was humiliated to see that it was Maisy who was talking to him, and now she would see how stupid he was as he chased the bouncing balls down the street. She laughed and he was granted the chance to see her face light up with joy as her dimples flashed a teasing smile.

"Hi, Maisy. Sorry, I'm not usually so clumsy."

"Oh, I think it's wonderful. How did you learn to do that, anyway?"

"My father taught me. He used to be in the circus," said Max, with a puffed up chest. He adjusted his suspenders and tucked in his shirt, then ran a hand over his slicked down hair, just to make sure the cowlick had not popped up again.

Maisy and Max walked and talked, and a bond was formed that day that was never to be broken. Earl watched from inside his house as they passed by, and a jealous rage reared its ugly head. He made a vow to make sure that Maisy would be his. He would make her like him somehow. Throughout the school years and summers ahead, Max and Maisy were often seen together, sitting on the dock, dangling their feet in the water as they talked about life and their hopes and dreams. Earl did his best to trail along, but the two considered him to be a pest and tried their best to avoid him. When they were fifteen they began stealing kisses behind a wood shed or a lilac bush that was tall enough to give them privacy for a moment. It was 1910 and

Maisy knew the traditional values of the time; it was wrong for a girl to kiss someone she wasn't married to, but she couldn't help it. She was hopelessly and totally in love with Max, and of course, Max had loved her since he first laid eyes on her two years ago. Fortunately, for the two, things did not move along too quickly, because the entire neighborhood had watchful eyes, and also because the young were not allowed outside at night after nine o'clock, which was the respectable time to retire for the night.

One hot day in June when Maisy and Max were sitting on a blanket in the park at Lake Michigan, Earl showed up. "Hi, mind if I join you?"

"Of course, not," said Maisy who was always polite. But behind Earl's back, she made a face at Max. Earl had been maturing over the last few months, and even though he was the same age as the other two, he was beginning to look more like a man. His shoulders were broadening out, his neck was getting thicker, and it was obvious that he had started to shave. Max still had his youthful look, with a face as smooth as a baby's, but the dark hair and complexion of his Romani roots were undeniable. He was extremely good-looking for a teen, and had nothing to worry about where the girls were concerned. The two boys were feeling competitive for the girl they both cared for. Earl bragged about his latest fishing haul. Max decided to show off his new trick to Maisy, and jumped up to juggle, which turned out to be a big mistake, because after a few minutes, Earl slid his hand over Maisy's and held it awhile. She looked at Earl in surprise, but she smiled and left her hand there. It was fun to be liked by two boys at once, she decided.

"Maisy," said Earl, "want to get some ice cream? I brought a dime with me."

"Okay," said Maisy. "How about you, Max? Are you coming?" She turned to the boy she had come with, hoping he would follow, too. It was flattering having two fellows around.

Max knew he had no money in his pocket, so he scuffed his foot in the dirt and said, "No, thanks. I have to get back. I promised my mother I would clean out the garage this afternoon. You two go ahead."

Earl was thrilled with his luck. He would have Maisy all to himself. Now Maisy wasn't too sure about this idea; it wasn't what she had planned at all. And she never wanted to hurt Max, because she suspected he didn't have any money. 'How can I be so cruel?' she wondered. This was supposed to be their picnic day, and now she and Earl had ruined it.

"I'll see you later, after you're finished with your chores, okay, Max?" She gave a little wave, and walked away with Earl. He tried to take her hand again, but she pulled it back, leaving him puzzled. He vowed to try once more later on. She had given him an opening, and he was not going to lose his chance again.

Maisy's experience with Earl that day was not so bad, after all. He was very attentive, and she decided it was nice to have a boy buy her ice cream. She wasn't particularly attracted to him, not like she was to Max, but she was young and trying to figure things out as she went along. When she was with Earl she enjoyed his company, but when she was with Max, she felt a tingle and a yearning that almost scared her. She decided Earl was safer, for now.

This back and forth between the two boys went on for several years. Maisy's heart was always for Max, but Earl was kind and attentive and she was not a person to say no to anyone, so when he asked her out, she went. And finally one night, in May of 1913, when Maisy and the boys had turned eighteen years old, everything changed.

Chapter Eight

It was Saturday, and Max was eagerly looking forward to taking Maisy out in the rowboat for an evening ride on the lake. The water was still and the sky was clear, so it would be a perfect time to view the moon. She had already said yes, and it was all he could think about the whole day. Max had been working with his father at the ice and coal company to help out with the family, so he had to turn over almost all of his earnings. And he tried to help out the family by purchasing his own clothing. He had been wanting to buy Maisy something special for her eighteenth birthday, but he had not been able to save enough for a purchase that was just right, and now there was no time to get to a store. He was so disappointed. When his father had questioned his bad mood, Max told him about his plans for Maisy's birthday. Edward really liked Maisy; he thought she was the perfect match for his son. Her light coloring, so much like Clara's, was a perfect complement to Max's dark brooding looks. Edward patted his son on his back, took a deep sigh, and went into his room. When he returned he was carrying a small box. He handed it to his questioning son.

"Max, my son, I was saving this for the right moment, and I believe this is the time, but only you will know for sure."

"What are you talking about, Pa?"

"In this box is the necklace that belonged to your mother. It used to glow with warmth whenever she wore it, but when she died it turned cold. I only handled it once after her death in an attempt to feel her through it, but her spirit was gone and the necklace was as cold as ice."

Max's eyes grew large as he realized what his father was saying. This was the ruby necklace that Edward had given to Clara on her birthday, the one he believed made her fall in love with him. The one he had been given by a fortune teller. Max had not been told about the mystical powers of the necklace, but he had always assumed there was more to the story than his father had told him. He opened the box slowly, and gazed upon it with awe. The box seemed to vibrate, the rubies and diamonds came to life and sparkled, but when Edward reached out a tentative hand to touch a stone, he felt nothing, and the rubies appeared lifeless and dull to his eyes. But what Max saw and felt was totally different. He felt warmth and life and an urgency he had never felt before. He threw his arms around his father, and cried. He cried for the loss of his mother, he cried for this generous man who had done something very difficult for him by bringing to mind his terrible loss, and he cried with happiness because he knew without a doubt that Maisy was going to be his.

"Oh, Pa, this is the best gift you could have ever given me. But why have you never shown this to me before?"

"The time was not right, son. You'll see why. You're eighteen and a man now; some things come with responsibility and today is one of those times, and this is one of those things."

"A necklace?"

"A very special necklace," said his father. "Treat it well, and it will do right by you. Trust me, you'll see."

"I'm not sure I understand, but I will do as you say. I'll treasure this gift always."

"Now, go get ready for your evening with Maisy, but be careful. If I'm right, and I'm not sure I am, something unexpected may change for you tonight. I'm proud of you, son. Now take precautions. Be gentle. But most of all, remember that love is a sacred trust. When you are allowed to share someone's heart and soul, you will have been given a true gift that will be with you for the rest of your life"

"Yes, Father, I will try to honor what you have said, even though I have no idea what it means."

Edward laughed out loud. "You will, boy, you will."

≈

Max found a piece of fabric and a ribbon in Lena's sewing box. He wrapped his package carefully, and then began to dress for the night. It was just a casual boat ride, they had gone on many before, but he wanted to look his very best for Maisy tonight. His father had recognized what a special time this would be for him, he had felt something that even Max had not been aware of, and now he was more excited than ever for Maisy to see his gift.

Max's tweed knickers were fashionable for boating and yard work, but the style was also worn by the wealthy who played golf. Max was glad that he had spent some of his money last year on this new fashion item, along with a new pair of suspenders, even though his father had been upset that he had not purchased something more 'practical.' He wore his high top socks which disappeared under the knee length pant leg, and then he covered his shoes with spats.   Once he added his tweed Kirby flat cap on top of his head, he was ready to go. Even though he wore this outfit every Sunday in the summer, he felt as if it was the first time.

Max walked nervously toward Maisy's house, the package clutched tightly in his hand. It sent a slight vibration up his arm, which puzzled him, but he didn't have time to question it now. He would meet her at her house, and then they would walk to the dock to his boat. When Max knocked nervously on the door, he was pleased that it opened within a few short seconds. Maisy didn't subscribe to etiquette of the day which dictated that the man should sit, in utter agony, with a young woman's father while waiting for his date to appear. Besides, there was no man at the house to wait with and her mother had been busy getting her ready with a last minute alteration.

The vision Max saw when the door was opened made him involuntarily take a step back, whereby he almost fell off the porch. When Maisy laughed, it sounded like a beautiful song to him. She was dressed in a lightweight cotton called lawn white. The dress was a new creation her mother had sewn for her as a birthday present. The gown was long with a flowing gossamer skirt which was cinched around her waist in a high position and held in place with a wide red satin ribbon. The sleeves were tight to her arm except at the shoulder area where they puffed out in a billowed cloud. The neckline was square with a slight bit of lace around it, exposing a portion of Maisy's chest, the sight of which had been previously denied to Max. Her large-brimmed hat sat on her head at a jaunty angle, and flaunted a huge feather on the side. There was a hatpin with a bright red stone on the end stuck through the hat to hold it firmly on her head, but it kept her hair hidden from view except for the nape of her neck, where a peek of her white blonde upswept hairdo was exposed. Small tendrils escaped and cascaded down her neck, moving in the gentle breeze. Her beauty sucked the breath out of him; he was unable to form a decent thought, and struggled to speak words which should have come naturally. Maisy noticed his distress, and worried that something was wrong, when she heard his voice choke out a sound that was unlike anything she had heard from Max in all of the years she had known him. It almost sounded like a stifled sob. And indeed it was.

"Maisy, you look -- so lovely, and – uh, happy birthday," he stuttered.

"Thank you, Max." She was very pleased with his reaction, because even though she looked like an angel, she had been having thoughts that were definitely not ladylike about Max. It puzzled her immensely, because she still felt a slight attraction to Earl. But here was Max before her, looking all grown up. There was slight nick on his chin where he had shaved, and splashed rosewater as an astringent. Maisy was very pleased, indeed. When she reached out to take Max's hand as he helped her down the porch steps, she experienced a warmth and tingle that traveled up her arm, and went straight to her heart. She sighed, and smiled happily. It was going to be a perfect evening.

Chapter Nine

The wind was dead calm, the sun was low in the sky, and the water of Lake Muskegon looked like glass. Max was thrilled to be sitting across from Maisy in the boat. He could study her every move as he rowed -- the tilt of her head, the grace with which she used her hands, and the way her pearly teeth flashed when she smiled. 'Why had he never noticed these things before?' he wondered. 'She's perfection.'

On the opposite end of the boat, Maisy was having similar thoughts about Max. She noticed how his hair had become darker as he had grown up; an intriguing curl escaped from his flat cap -- which he had set on the back of his head -- and the runaway lock rested on his forehead. He had rolled up his sleeves when he began to row the boat, so she was able to watch his muscles play on his forearms, which had gotten thicker in the last few months – they were a man's arm, developed by the heavy lifting of coal and ice. She could tell that his thighs looked strong under the fabric of his knickers, and she blushed when she realized what she had been thinking about. They moved silently away from the shore, not going out too far, in case a large ship came in through the channel from Lake Michigan, but just far enough so that they were out of the earshot of the evening walkers who would be strolling along the shoreline on this beautiful night. He had a lot to say, and he didn't want anyone who might hear to have influence on his lovely boating partner.

"Maisy, have you thought about your life, at all, now that you're eighteen? You know, the future and all?"

"Yes, I have, actually. And I'm more perplexed than ever. I don't want to be a seamstress for the rest of my life, working in my mother's house. But that's all I know how to do."

"You know how we've always talked about the circus?"

"You've talked about the circus, you mean."

Max laughed. "I guess, it *was* me, but you enjoyed the talk of traveling, too, didn't you?"

"Yes, of course, there's so much of this country I want to see, but I haven't a clue how that will ever happen for me. You have options. I'll be stuck here in Muskegon for the rest of my life." She pouted prettily.

Max wondered how far he should go with his thoughts, but he was too far away from Maisy to broach the subject he had been longing to bring up. "I've already talked to my father about leaving someday."

"You have?" Maisy felt panic begin to set in. What would she do without him? He had been a constant in her life for six years, now. Her eyes got big and began to water, but because the light was dimming Max had not noticed how upset she was.

"I've always wanted to join the circus like my parents did, but the more I think of it, the more I'm inclined to become a vaudevillian."

"Like Buster?"

"Yes, I plan to talk to him when he comes back home next month. He should be able to give me some good pointers."

"My goodness, Max. I had no idea it had come to this, already. What will I do if you leave me?" Now she began to cry, her shoulders shaking with soft sobs.

Max left his oars and scooted over to sit next to her on her seat. She put her head on his shoulder, and felt the warmth of his arm as he wrapped it around her tiny waist. The gift-wrapped package was vibrating stronger than ever. He felt the time was now or never, so just before the sun dipped below the horizon and the moon rose higher in the sky, he pulled out his birthday gift.

"Please don't cry, Maisy. I have something special for you."

"You do?" Maisy dabbed at her nose with a delicate handkerchief she had retrieved from her satin drawstring bag.

"Of course, I'd never forget to give you a birthday gift. It's not wrapped too pretty, but once you see what's inside, I'll explain the contents."

Max held his breath with anticipation as Maisy opened her package. When she lifted the ruby and diamond necklace from its case, she gasped. The moonlight caught the stones and sent a display of sparkles that danced around the boat and on top of the water. At that exact moment the sky began to glow with a glorious sunset of reds and golds, highlighting the luxuriousness of the stones.

"Max! I've never seen anything like this. How – where – is it real?"

"I believe they are, but my father never had it looked at by a jeweler. It was my mother's, and it meant a lot to both of my parents. My father gave it to her on her birthday when they first fell in love. He offered it to me to give to the love of my life." Max's voice began to quiver. He had said it out loud – the love of his life – and he knew the moment the words were out that it was true. He would never love another like he loved Maisy.

"Love, Max? What are you saying? You love me?"

"I do, Maisy Abernathy. I have loved you since the moment I first saw you in pigtails in Miss Colton's classroom. But tonight my heart is bursting with love for you." Max took both of Maisy's gloved hands in his and looked into her teary eyes. "May I place the necklace on you?"

"Please do." Maisy's breath was uneven and her heart felt like it would come through her chest. "How will I ever explain this gift to Mama? She'll never let me keep it."

"It will be our secret, Maisy," he whispered in her ear, "my father will never tell. He understands the necklace better than I, and I see now that I am just beginning to learn about it myself."

The moment the necklace touched Maisy's neck, it automatically settled into the place around the hollow of her throat. It pulsed its secret message and warmed her through and through. Maisy gazed longingly at Max, and without hesitation leaned in for a kiss, a kiss longer and far more passionate than they had ever experienced before. When the kiss was over, she looked into Max's beautiful brown eyes, and knew she would never let anyone tear her away from the man she loved. The couple sat head to head under the shining moon, until the settling dew reminded them that they had been out much too long. It wasn't difficult to row back to shore in the dark because a moonbeam showed them the way with the help of the glittering colors dancing off of the ruby necklace at Maisy's throat.

When they got back to the dock, Max took her hand and reluctantly helped her out of the boat. It would be difficult for him to return her to her mother. As they walked along the path to her front door, Max pulled Maisy behind a tall blooming forsythia bush. He kissed her the way he had always dreamed about kissing her and was surprised that she returned his passion. Maisy wound her arms around his neck and found herself pushing her body up tight to his, something no self-respecting girl would ever do. If this was wrong, she didn't care. All she cared about was satisfying a craving she had never known she had. Max ran his hands down her back, back up to her necklace which was hot to the touch, and then he tightened his hold. Maisy could barely breathe, his passion was so strong – he was so strong. He artfully slid a hand downward so he could trail his fingers over one breast and he was thrilled when she did not slap his hand away; in fact she seemed to want more as a small sigh escaped and she arched her back.

"Max, Max, I love you so," she gasped. "But please, we must stop. Mama will come out soon; she'll be looking for me. I don't want her to find me in a mess. We have to stop." She pushed gently back.

"Yes, yes, you're right."

Maisy moaned when the space between them became too much for her to bear. "Please, don't stop, Max." She moved back in to taste his lips once again.

Max was breathing heavily. Understanding, now, what his father had warned him about, he said, "We must. I'm sorry, but we must. Here, let me take off the necklace. Maybe you can hide it somewhere."

The moment the necklace was removed, their urgency was dampened slightly, but there was enough left behind for the young lovers to take home with them and dream about later. When they stepped out from behind the bush, they were surprised to see that there was someone who had been watching and knew what they were doing all along. Their attempts at secrecy had been to no avail. He was standing perfectly still and was glaring at them with clenched fists.

"Earl! Earl Shaeffer, what are you doing there?"

Chapter Ten

"Get your hands off her!" Earl yelled. He advanced forward as if to strike Max.

Maisy shouted, "Earl, no! It's okay. I love Max. We love each other."

Max who was ready to defend Maisy's honor, was held back by his beloved with her gloved hand on his chest. He was surprised and happy that she had so readily told someone of their love. Earl was in a stance with fists balled tightly, ready to strike. How could Max treat his lovely Maisy like that, like a paid woman in the red light district! As the two men confronted each other with raised voices, Maisy's mother came out to see what was going on.

"Maisy, are you all right?"

"Yes, Mother, I'll explain when I get inside."

Earl was not about to let this affront to the girl of his dreams go unnoticed. "Mrs. Abernathy, I came upon Max accosting Maisy. I thought it was my duty to protect her."

With a hand clasped to her chest, Maisy's mother gasped, "Is that true, Maisy?"

Sensing the fact that the whole neighborhood would soon find out what had gone on in the bushes, Maisy took matters into her own hands. "This is not the way I planned to tell you, Mother, but Max just proposed, and we were – well, we were sealing it with a kiss." Maisy glanced at Max and gave a slight nod hoping he would follow her lead. Max burst out with a wide grin. He really *had* wanted to propose after that last kiss, because he could not imagine not being able to finish what they had started. He might have chosen a more romantic setting than her mother's front yard, though, he thought.

Earl was shocked. He was sure that a marriage proposal was not the case at all. It couldn't be. Maisy was meant to be his!

Mrs. Abernathy stepped out to hug her lovely daughter and soon to be son-in-law. She had suspected something was about to happen between the two kids this evening, especially since Maisy was eighteen now. "Well, congratulations! Come in and tell me all about it. Earl, would you care to join us?"

"No, thank you, ma'am. I was heading home. I'll just be on my way." He tipped his hat and moved away into the night. As Earl left the happy family behind, Max could have sworn he saw steam coming out of his ears. Max laughed out loud. Unfortunately, Earl heard it, and knew the guffaw was about him.

Max sneaked a kiss on Maisy's cheek on the way into the house, and whispered, "Quick thinking, Maisy. Genius. But I would have gotten around to it anyway, in another day or two." He held her hand tightly, slowing their pace down behind her mother.

"Oh, Max. Do you think I was too forward? We can break it off in a while if you want."

"Maisy, Maisy, Maisy, my sweet thing. I love you. You're mine forever and always." The ruby necklace was on fire, sending heat right through the case. Max wrapped both of their hands around the box, and they smiled sheepishly, knowing what was to come. Max nuzzled her neck, and whispered, "Let's save this for the wedding night."

Maisy nodded weakly, and blushed hotly in the moonlight.

Word spread quickly of the engagement, and everyone but Earl agreed it was a perfect match. 'We all knew Max and Maisy would be together one day,' they commented. 'It was inevitable,' they said. When The Keaton family and the rest of the 200 vaudevillians arrived in June, there were even more congratulations. And when Max and Buster were alone for a few moments, Max explained his desire to join the vaudeville troupe. Buster agreed that he was more than ready. When Max showed him a few new moves he had learned, Buster was impressed. He made suggestions here and there that would enhance his act, and as Max practiced throughout the rest of June, July, and August, he got better and better. He was now able to throw the balls extremely high while juggling three or more at a time and all the while never dropping a one. He taught himself to spin a plate on a stick held in his mouth while he continued to juggle, throwing balls behind his back and under a leg. Finally, he felt that he was ready to perform in front of an audience, so Buster secured a spot for him in the practice run of the show that the actors and vaudevillians performed for the locals every summer.

Max was nervous but excited. Maisy had made him a wonderful costume, a black tuxedo with sequins on the lapels; he felt so professional. He was eager and ready to go. The whole town was in the audience the night of the show, including his father who was about ready to pop his buttons with his pride-filled chest. His son was on stage with Buster Keaton, well-known for the prat falls he could take and his comedic stone-faced genius; Mush Rawls, a famous blackface comedian and ventriloquist; and Samaroff and Sonia, who did a dancing, acrobatic dog act and who had recently performed for the King of England.

Max performed without a hitch, never once dropping a ball, and to his very own amazement, he received a standing ovation from the local townspeople. From that moment on, he was hooked. Buster, of course, was the star of the show, but he was very generous with his praise for Max's act. He encouraged the young couple to join them on tour; it would be fun to have a buddy from home with him. They could play ball whenever they had some time off, he said. Maisy had to admit to feeling so much pride for Max. Her very own husband-to-be would be famous one day, and she decided right then and there that she would follow him to the ends of the Earth.

Following the mid-afternoon performance, as the couple walked to the dock for a boat ride, openly holding hands, they discussed what went on backstage and Max told Maisy about things she had not ever heard before. He told her about how they put on exaggerated makeup so their features could be seen from the farthest row back, and he described the important role the seamstresses had. They made all of the costumes for the group, he said, and they were right there through the whole thing in case of a popped button and ripped seam. They actually repaired the costumes sometimes while they were still on the actor's body, he told her.

Maisy was amazed. She had never thought of herself as being a part of this colorful new world, but now she could see that there was possibly a place for her, too. When Max asked that she marry him *before* the vaudevillians left for the summer and go with him to their first stop in Chicago, where the acts would gather and the new acts would audition for a coveted spot on the bill, she agreed with a happy squeal.

"Yes, yes, yes," she said. "Let's go home right now and tell Mama."

"She might not be too happy," said Max, nervously. "My father is ready for this, but she isn't. It could be a shock."

"But we need to do it now, while she is still impressed with what she saw this afternoon."

"You're right. Let's do it. There's a whole new world waiting for us, Maisy Abernathy."

"Well, soon it'll be Maisy Woods. Much better, don't you think? Mr. and Mrs. Maxwell Woods." They kissed in broad daylight, at the edge of the water, and didn't care one bit what anyone thought.

Chapter Eleven

The wedding was meant to be a small affair in Maisy's neighbor's gazebo by the water's edge. Only Max's father, step-mother, Lena -- who highly disapproved of the young couples' plan to leave town – Max's step-brother and step-sister, and Maisy's mother would be attending. But no one anticipated that the whole community of Bluffton would turn out to view the wedding from the street.

Maisy wore a simple but elegant gown her mother had painstaking sewn for her only daughter's wedding. It was cut in a loose flowing style of imported lace with three layers in varying length, in a Roman or Greek style of old; it fit the bride to perfection. The bodice was wrapped with a satin cummerbund and the neckline laid simply across the collarbone allowing for the ruby necklace to take center stage, the rubies being a perfect match for the red roses the bride carried. Maisy wore a gossamer headpiece, similar to a night cap that trailed a sheer veil down her back, specially made so the groom could view her beautiful white-gold hair. The necklace was explained as a gift Edward had purchased in Europe for Max's mother, Clara, and had been held in trust to be passed down on this occasion. But only the young couple, and Edward, knew of its power. Max was more than a little embarrassed when his father nodded at the gems that Maisy was wearing and winked.

When the final vows were spoken and the couple sealed the marriage with a kiss, the crowd erupted in a cheer, and then the impromptu party began, impromptu as far as the wedding party was concerned, because the Bluffton crowd had been scheming and planning for weeks. A parade began to form with the bride and groom being carried in a buggy led by two matching horses belonging to one of the vaudevillians. They were followed by singers, belly dancers, acrobats, and dogs dressed up in their show time finery. They marched around the village blocks, and those who had not attended the wedding came out to cheer them on. It was about as close to a circus parade as Max had ever gotten. The young couple could not have felt more loved – except for one man standing on the sidelines with anything but happiness on his face – Earl Schaeffer.

After the wedding Maisy and Max went back to her mother's house to stay for their first night of wedded bliss until they left to go to Chicago the following day. Maisy's mother played cards with friends until late into the night, allowing the bride and groom some privacy. And it was a good thing she did, because she would have been shocked at the sounds of passionate ecstasy coming from Maisy's room. The necklace had warmed Maisy and Max all through the wedding, vibrating until they thought they would go mad until they could be alone. It was to the point that they could barely keep their hands off of each other, but manners of the time dictated otherwise. They were the picture of decorum until they closed the door to the house, and then they began to kiss and explore without any fear or shame. Once their clothing was removed there were no boundaries. Max was more than pleased with the enthusiasm for lovemaking that his new bride was displaying. And Maisy was thrilled with the feeling of Max's body next to hers, skin to skin, as she had dreamed since the first time she had put on the necklace. The two virgins consummated their union in perfect harmony. They were sleeping soundly, naked in each other's arms, when Maisy's mother tiptoed into her house way past midnight.

Maisy yearned for more lovemaking the following morning, and Max obliged her in as quiet a way as possible, then he said, "I think we'd better slip off your necklace, Maisy, or I won't make it to Chicago without a stop for more – you know."

Maisy laughed at what felt like their secret, the secret of two people completely in love feeling as if they were the only ones in the whole world who had ever felt such a connection. There was a need, now, that had been unleashed, and as long as they had each other, it would never disappear.

"Max, I love you so much," said the beauty with the messy white hair. She trailed her finger over his chest, lovingly touching the dark down that extended downward.

Max ran his fingers over what he considered to be a gift meant for him alone, marveling at the female body and its mysteries, then he unclasped the necklace and they tucked it safely away in its box. They pushed it to the bottom of the suitcase they would carry to Chicago, and then they began to get ready to join the others at the train station. Today, the first day of their life together, would be the beginning of their big adventure.

The train chugged into the station in Muskegon, leaving behind a cloud of smoke to decorate the morning sky. The vaudevillians were on the platform lugging huge amounts of baggage with them; there was teasing and camaraderie as the performers all felt the excitement of the new season. It was everything Max had ever dreamed of. He was part of a wild and colorful bunch of people who were more than ready to accept him into their way of life, and besides all of that, he had his bride at his side. There had been tears of goodbye, but everyone knew the vaudevillians came back to Bluffton every summer, so the parting was not as painful as it might have been. Max and Maisy had already turned over their baggage to the stewards, and were about to board with the others, when Maisy heard her name called out. She turned to see a miserable Earl standing there with his hat in his hand, holding a bunch of wildflowers.

Max stepped forward, blocking Maisy from Earl with his body. "What do you want?" he snarled.

"Well, um, I -- Maisy and Max, I just wanted to say I'm sorry for the way I have behaved. I see that you two are very happy, and I'm glad for you. But I have one thing to say." He turned to Maisy alone and said softly,

"If you ever need me for anything, and I mean anything, I'll be there for you. If you feel like this isn't the life for you, and you want to return, I'll come to Chicago or wherever you are to get you."

Max stepped closer to Earl, a snarl on his face and clenched fists at his side ready to punch his foe in the nose, but Maisy intervened, not wanting to start something in front of the others.

"Thank you, Earl. I know you are well-meaning, but I love Max. We're married now, and I will go with him wherever he chooses to take us," Maisy smiled kindly, knowing Earl was in pain, but it would never change her mind about her husband. "We can still be friends, can't we? And we'll see you next summer, same as always, okay?"

Earl nodded, shoved the flowers in her hand, and walked away a broken man, knowing she was lost to him forever.

Maisy looked up at Max, and said, "I feel badly for him. We were such good friends once."

Max simply grunted, "I feel nothing."

≈

The next few weeks were a whirlwind of activity for the new couple. Once they were settled into the boarding house that all of their friends usually stayed at, they had to learn their way around the city. The size of Chicago was overwhelming at times, but it didn't take long before they were able to learn the major streets they needed, and soon they had a favorite route to restaurants and auditions. Maisy had packed a small supply of needles and thread along with her darning egg. When the word spread of her sewing expertise, the vaudevillians began coming to her for a quick fix on their clothing and costumes, if they had had a mishap during the day, so at least Maisy was bringing in a small income.

Max on the other hand, was struggling. Each day he would get up, full of energy, ready to prove his worth to the troupes in town. He auditioned many times, but each time was told they already had a juggler or a juggling team that would work on stage with two or more people moving balls, and even knives, between them. He would come home so discouraged that it broke Maisy's heart, so after a nice warm meal, which was provided by the boarding house, she would lock their door and slowly and suggestively put on the necklace. They never got tired of having Maisy wear the necklace. They were young, with energy to spare, and their sexual appetite for each other was insatiable. But after the lovemaking, when Maisy was sleeping happily by his side, Max would lie awake and wonder what went wrong. Why could he not get a job? He was told he was good, but not good enough, something he always left out of the conversation when telling Maisy about his day. The best he could hope for, he was told, was to be hired as a standby in case someone else got sick. They would give him a call if needed. He was ashamed and humiliated that he was not able to provide for his wife.

After several weeks most of the actors began leaving Chicago; they were going on tour around the country – some even to Europe. They patted Max on the back and said how sorry they were he was not coming with them this year. Buster felt especially bad for encouraging his friend to come along in the first place. There were plenty of shows that remained permanently in Chicago, so Maisy and Max decided to stay behind and try for a gig in the 'Windy City.' A few others stayed with them, because there was always a need for an act on the stage there, but nothing came Max's way. Luckily, Maisy was able to secure a job as a seamstress for a local alteration business. Their small income was just enough to pay the rent, and since they were provided with breakfast and supper, they survived on two meals a day, and were thankful for a soft bed and a warm place to sleep.

The problem began when some of the guys asked Max to go out with them for a beer at the local pub. He first responded that he didn't have any money for a beer, but two of the guys offered to buy him a glass. "Come on," they said. "You deserve it. You've been working so hard. Get away from the missus for one night." Max had to admit it did sound tempting, and his logic was that maybe he would meet someone there that would want to hire him. He certainly wasn't going to make any connections in their room. He had to be out with people, he told himself. His first night out with the men was so relaxing. 'It was a chance to laugh,' he told Maisy. 'It was just what I needed,' he said. When they asked him again, he readily agreed, this time without consulting her first.

In the beginning, Maisy had agreed that Max should have a little fun. She usually had a pile of mending to do, because besides her day job at the alteration business, she also still took in mending at the boarding house. The owner had hired her to repair torn sheets, and to be on call for the other paying boarders who came and went throughout the week. A little time alone in the evening sitting beside an open window was calming for her; it was a time when she could relax and reflect on her life and the quiet community in Muskegon she had left behind. But soon she began to get lonely at night. Max was coming home later and later each time he went out. And each time he came home a little drunker than the last. At first when he came home, smelling of beer, it was exciting for Maisy. He had a swagger that was fascinating, and he flirted in a more sexual way. She would put on the necklace, and in combination with the uninhibited feelings the alcohol produced in Max, their lovemaking was even more enhanced, if that was possible. But when he started to stumble in at night and collapse on the bed, passing out sometimes before he even greeted her, she knew they were in trouble. On those nights, even the necklace could not tempt the man she loved so dearly.

Maisy knew it was time for a talk, and she also knew that Max was not going to like what she had to say. "Max, before you go out tonight, can I talk to you?"

"Of course, love. What do you want to talk about?"

"I know you feel that these evenings out are making contacts and friends that can help you, but I just don't see how. Can you tell me about anyone who has given you a lead?"

"Well, no, most of them are in the same boat I am. Finding work on the stage is much more difficult than I thought it would be. I'm sorry, Maisy, but I seem to be getting nowhere."

"That's what I thought. And how are you getting money for all of the alcohol that you are drinking?"

"I'm usually able to buy one glass, thanks to your sewing, but then I play cards for the rest. It turns out that I'm pretty good at poker." He grinned at the fact that he had found a talent he had not known he had. "There's always a game going on, so I play for drinks, but sometimes I win money. I'm hoping to win more than I drink tonight, so I can bring something home to you." He chuckled sexily, and pulled her close to him. How he loved to nuzzled her neck.

"Max, I'm serious. This isn't what we came here to do. It's almost Christmas. I'd like to go home to see my mother. I don't like the sound of her letters. I believe she's hiding something. And I was thinking maybe we should change our plans. Maybe vaudeville isn't for us."

Max angrily pushed Maisy away from him. "No, it's not time to give up yet. This is all I've ever wanted, you know that. You knew it when you married me."

"Yes, Max, I did. But I didn't plan on spending my days sewing, living in a one-room boarding house, and spending my nights alone." Maisy was crying now. She cried for their situation, she cried for the changes that had taken place in Max, and she cried because she was the cause of their first fight. If only she had not brought up his drinking and nights out. She vowed never to do it again. She apologized and kissed him over and over, until he relented, tossing her on the bed for a quick tumble before leaving for the night.

Chapter Twelve

Everyone complained about the winter of 1913 in Chicago. It was colder than normal, they said, and the unending wind seemed to cut right through them. Max and Maisy didn't seem to notice and wondered what all the fuss was about. It was cold, yes, and windy, but that's what winter was every year. The winter winds generally blew from west to east, away from Chicago and Wisconsin, traveling across the water to the west side of Michigan, which is where both Maisy and Max were born and raised. They were used to the icy cold blasts which had gained speed as they traveled across the wide expanse of water.

Maisy was homesick after only a few short months of marriage; she really wanted to catch a train home for Christmas, but of course, there was no money. She would have to be satisfied with the letters that arrived regularly in order to keep up with the news. In the latest one her mother had casually written that she had not been feeling well lately. She declared it to be a long lasting cold, but Maisy knew better. She could tell by the tone of her words. Maisy wrote a long letter to her mother, about their experiences in such a huge city. She tried to be upbeat so she told about customers she dealt with and repeated some of the funny quips of the vaudevillians. She wrote about Max's attempts to gain a spot on the vaudeville stage, but she never wrote about his failures, or his drinking and despair.

Maisy was convinced they needed to go home, not only to see her mother, but also for Max's sake. She thought if she could get him back to more normal surroundings, he would become the man she knew he was deep inside – kind, caring, generous, and excited about life. This man she saw after his nights out with the guys was not someone she would ever have dreamed Max would become. She tried discussing his behavior with some of the other wives. The women sometimes gathered together in the evening, gossiping and smoking -- Ivy had begun smoking, also, in order to fit in. They laughed when she squinted her eyes to avoid the curling smoke, so one of the women had offered her a long cigarette holder she had been given and had never used. It made Maisy feel as if the new habit she was developing wasn't quite so filthy. With the holder in her hand, she felt like high-society; she felt like they had made it. While she was smoking she was more relaxed when she discussed her problem about Max and his drinking, but it seemed she was the only one who was worried about her husband. They all accepted the drinking as part of what a man did and who he was. If they complained about a lack of money because it was spent on alcohol and gambling, they never showed it to her. Dealing with a man's strange ways was laughed off as part of life. Maisy would smile and agree with them, but inside she was hurting. She felt alone in a world of performers and actors who held a different outlook on life than she did. She just did not understand them, plain and simple.

The weeks turned into months, and before anyone knew it, it was spring. The air was fresher, the sky was bluer, and the sun was warmer, which was very uplifting, but Maisy missed the bird songs, the blooming trees, and the activity of a small town. Chicago was on Lake Michigan, and being near water had always been important to her, but she was on the wrong side of the pond. She never adjusted to the fact that the sun rose where the water met the horizon. She had spent her whole life watching the sun *set* over the big lake. Everything about Chicago was different, seemed wrong, and she worried that she would never adapt, and wasn't even sure she wanted to.

As their original group began to gather in Chicago after their travels were completed, and everyone was making plans to return to Muskegon in June, Maisy began to get excited. She would finally be able to go home. But one evening when Max was getting ready to go out, and Maisy was rambling on about home and when they would leave, and what they would take, Max blew up.

"What in the world are you talking about? We can't go home!"

"What do you mean?" she asked, nervously. He was angry – angrier than she had ever seen him.

"Money, woman, money! We have none!" he yelled."

"Why, surely, we can scrape up enough for the train ticket. Once we get there, we can live with Mama, rent free. She'll be happy for our help in exchange. I know she is not feeling well, yet."

"Maisy, you're such a fool. We have no money. I have no job. I've never even performed on the stage once! I will not return to Bluffton a failure."

"Max, you're not a failure. Our break just hasn't come along, yet," consoled Maisy.

"It doesn't matter what you think. We're staying here in Chicago. There are a few shows that continue through the summer and some will need an act to replace the people who leave for their summer resorts. I have to try to get one of those spots. If I can, maybe one of them will notice me, and want to keep me on in the fall. It's my only chance." Max gripped Maisy by both shoulders. His anger was so great that he wanted to shake her into understanding him.

"All right, but if it doesn't work out, and you can't find something after the group has returned to Michigan, then I think we should go, too. We can still have all of July and August at home, right?" she asked, with tears in her eyes.

Max looked at his lovely young wife's hopeful expression, her face framed by her soft hair, looking for all the world like an angel -- her huge blue eyes so full of trust. She had always believed in him and here he was, hurting his bride, his precious girl. What was wrong with him, he wondered. He was such a fool. He had everything he ever really wanted in Maisy. His world would be nothing without her. She was the one that had held them together since they arrived. He owed her everything. He made a promise to himself, then and there, that tonight would be his last night of poker. If he didn't win anything, he would find a regular job in order to save enough money to get her home for the summer. He softened his tone and released his grip. "Yes, my darling girl, we will go home then. I promise," he said, moving his body closer to hers. "I'm such a fool. I don't want to make you sad, but most of all, I hate to see you cry. Come here."

He pulled her to his lap, and cradled her head on his chest, while stroking her back. Then he whispered softly, "Can you wear the necklace for me when I get home, Maisy? I promise I'll be ready for it and you. Okay?"

"Okay, Max."

"I love you, you know."

"I love you, too." And just like that, Max was back to the man she knew and loved. Now if he could only hold to his promise to not return home drunk. Maisy sighed happily at the thought of what was to come. Once she put on the rubies and diamonds again, everything would be okay, she was sure of it.

$$\approx$$

The pub was not as full as it was on some nights, but Max was able to find a few friends to sit with. Most were not with the performing troupes, but were locals he had met since he had been coming regularly. His circle of friends had changed considerably. They were gamblers, more than drinkers. A few men gambled as a profession, but drinking interfered with their ability to read body language and keep track of cards. They liked nothing better than seeing Max show up, getting him drunk, and then taking whatever money he had earned off of the others. He was an easy mark, and he never seemed to catch on. It was part of his small town innocence, they said as they laughed behind his back.

Tonight was no different than the others, except for one thing -- Max had decided not to drink as much. He wanted his head clear, so he could make more money than usual and walk away with a full pocket. He would sip slowly and make it look like he was always drinking. No one ever actually counted the number of glasses he consumed. He would pretend to be drunk, so they would think they had the upper hand, and then he would swoop in for the kill. He thought it was a perfect plan, but the men that were there that night were no dummies. They were rough characters, and they would not be played.

The night started out with Max and his friends playing a friendly game as usual. As Max began to win and his streak continued, he became more and more aggressive with his bets. He felt sure about himself for the first time in a long time. And when he had a stash in front of him, and his friends had decided to quit playing, he moved over to a higher stakes table and asked to join in. It was exactly what the vultures had been waiting for. They smiled at each other and wondered who would be the lucky one to take every dime Max had.

And that's exactly what they did. It wasn't long before Max had lost everything, and then some, to a guy named Bernie Shortcake. Bernie had allowed him to continue playing to try to recoup his losses on the promise that he would pay him what he owed the next night.

It wasn't until after the rough guys left, when the bartender said to Max, 'Don't you know who that is? I tried to warn ya,' that Max began to get worried. What the bartender told him next was quite a surprise; he learned that Bernie Shortcake was a Chicago tough guy, a member of Big Jim Colosimo's South Side gang, called The Chicago Outfit. And the other four Max had been playing with were members, also. This gang had been around since 1909 when territories were established in Chicago and criminal activities began to escalate in the area. It would eventually grow and reorganize, and by 1919 Big Jim's nephew, Johnny Torrio would bring Al Capone into the mix who would eventually take over the rum-running operation during Prohibition, and be instrumental in the murder of Big Jim Colosimo.

Max had a much bigger problem on his hands than he originally thought. He not only owed someone a huge amount of money, but this person was a connected man; and therefore, it was not a good idea to be on his bad side. And the worst part of it all was that Max was flat broke, and there was nowhere to get any money. Maisy's wages for the week would not even make a dent. They were as poor as a church mouse, as Maisy's mother used to say. There was only one thing they owned that they could pawn. As soon as the idea came to him, Max knew what he had to do. It would be painful for both him and Maisy, but if what the bartender said was true, it would literally save his life. The necklace was the key to it all. But how would he tell Maisy?

The walk home was almost unbearable. He knew she would see trouble on his face the moment he entered the house; she could always read him like a book. The best part was that a storm was rolling in and the strong winds blasted his face and sobered him up. He decided that truth was the only option, but when Max opened the door, ready to tell his perfect, beautiful wife what had happened, she was lying on their bed, a sweet smile on her face, waiting to welcome him home. She was totally naked, except for the necklace which was sparkling and glowing like no other night. Its brilliance lured him in as always, but this time it was with a passion of a different nature. There *was* love, excitement, and lust, but it was wrapped up in sadness and disappointment and failure. His emotions were swirling wildly -- he needed Maisy more than ever, and she was happy to oblige. He needed her kisses and her loving murmurs. He needed to know she still loved him, because he was so afraid when he told her what he was about to do with the gift he had lovingly given her on her eighteenth birthday, she would never forgive him. He simply needed her.

When the drops of perspiration were still glistening on their bodies, and the glow of the summer moon coming through the window created shadows on their skin, Max confessed to what had happened tonight. He told her about the card game that escalated into something much more dangerous than he had ever been a part of before. He explained that he was now afraid for his life, and maybe hers, too. 'These are dangerous people,' he said. 'Chicago is a dangerous town.'

"But Max, what can we do?" asked Maisy, now terrified for her husband. "We have nothing. We can't pay up!"

Max looked at the love of his life, and said softly, "We have one thing, Maisy." He reached out and touched it. For one second, Max noticed the gems dimming, but when Maisy responded, they glowed brighter than all the stars in the sky.

Maisy's eyes welled with tears, as she assessed the trouble they were in. "Oh, honey, I know this is special to you," she said as she placed her hand on the stones herself, "but it's just a necklace. We don't need it to love each other. We loved each other before we had it, didn't we?"

"Yes, but not like this. And it was a gift from my father to my mother. It was meant for me and you. It's always been ours alone, that's why we've kept it a secret. I can't bear the fact that someone else might use it the same way we have."

"Oh, my sweet man, we have no other choice. It *is* very special, I've never questioned that, but maybe it was never meant to be with us for our entire life."

"That might be right, but after we were married, and we had discovered its powers, I went to my father to ask more about the necklace. I never told you because I thought you would be embarrassed about the subject of our lovemaking being discussed with him."

"Oh, you didn't! How could you!"

"Don't worry. I didn't go into details. By the look on his face, I didn't need to. I'm sure the rubies responded the same way to him and my mother. Anyway, the story he told me was that when the gypsy lady gave it to him, she said, 'This belongs to you. I have been waiting for you for a long time. I have only been the caretaker.' It puzzled me then, but now I think I understand. I think this necklace belongs to my family, it's been around for generations, and if I give it away, I'll have no chance of ever passing it on. I'll be a failure once more in my responsibilities."

"But if you don't do this, you won't be around to produce any offspring to pass it to. You have no choice."

Max raised his eyebrows. Maisy could always cut right through all of the muck to solve a problem. She was right, it didn't matter if he kept the necklace or not; all that mattered was that he stayed alive and protected Maisy.

"Tomorrow, I'll go back there with the necklace. I'll offer it to him directly, or ask if he would rather have me pawn it, and return with the money. I think I know the answer."

"That's a very wise decision, my darling, but what do you say we use the special power of the necklace one last time, because after tonight we'll be on our own."

The stones glowed as they warmed their hearts through with anticipation. That night Max could not get enough of tasting Maisy's lips and touching her soft skin. The electricity between them was more powerful than ever, and their lovemaking felt fresh and new as it soared to new heights.

Chapter Thirteen

The beating spring rain was relentless all morning, only to be joined by a powerful wind in the afternoon. This was not the normal routine that Mother Earth had worked out so well. Usually, strong gusts came first in March blowing off the straggling dead leaves which were left clutching to their branches for dear life. It was important that they be removed in order to make room for the fresh new buds. The earth would be pounded with huge amounts of water in order to saturate and prepare the previously frozen ground for the new growth that was to come in April. As the new blooms on the trees dropped their petals in May, and the now soft breeze carried the seeds they produced for the cycle of life to begin, the gentle rains took their turn. With the steady rains, the seeds would be carefully patted down into the soil where they could sprout roots, anchoring the wet seed pods as they popped open and sent up new green shoots ready to become a tree or flower, which in turn would house and feed the birds, bees, and other small critters. All of this wonderment happened without the help of man. That was the order of things and what was supposed to occur. But this year was different, because everything seemed out of sync. The gentle rain which was supposed to fall in the month of April and May was actually beating the earth to death, killing new growth the moment it appeared. It was a cold, wet rain similar to what was usually produced in the fall, and it brought with it a driving blast of frigid air.

Max walked bent over trying to protect himself from the driving wet force, his collar popped up in a useless effort to stop the water from going down his neck. By the time he arrived at the pub, he was drenched to the skin; the only place that was warm was the small area next to the package in his pocket. He opened the door and stepped into the darkness of the room. Standing there a moment to adjust his eyes, he saw the man he was looking for leaning against the bar, his cigar clutched in his teeth, a curl of smoke circling upward, as he talked to a man on his left. Max tentatively stepped forward not wanting to interrupt Bernie Shortcake and cause him to get upset, but at the same time needing to get this over with.

When Bernie noticed Max, he spun around with a big grin on his face. He could tell he was about to get his payday, and that made him happy. Contrary to what Max had been told, Bernie was a teddy bear, unless he was betrayed, and since Max had no plan to do anything like that, he was really quite safe. But Max didn't know the soft side of Bernie, and he began to shake with fear. He prayed he could convince Bernie to accept what he had to offer. In his opinion the necklace was worth much more than his debt, but he wondered if Bernie would see it that way.

"Hello, Bernie. How are you?"

"I'm great now that you're here. I see you caught a few raindrops, there. You need to get yourself a ride.

'Course if you keep losing at the table you'll never get one, huh?" He slapped the table at his own joke, and the men around him joined in the laughter.

"You're probably right," said Max humbly, "I'm not as good at this game as I thought. I came to settle my debt, and then I'm done with gambling forever."

"Really, kid? I kinda doubt that, but we'll see. What have you got for me?"

"Can we sit at the table over here? It's sort of private."

"Okay, kid. I don't mind, but I hope you brought me cash. That's all I want."

"Here let me pull out this chair for you, Bernie. You see, what I have is better than money."

Bernie's eyes narrowed. "Nothin's better than money," he growled, his hand patting the butt of his pistol.

"Just give me a chance, okay?" Max reached in his pocket and touch the wrapped necklace. It gave him a small electric shock, and he jerked back his hand.

"What is that? Is it alive?"

"No," laughed Max. "I stuck myself with a pin. Here, here it is." He removed the necklace from the handkerchief Maisy had rolled it in, and laid it out in front of Bernie, with his hand still on it, protectively touching it. It glowed and sparkled for Max, catching the gaslights which were shining overhead. "Now, I know you wanted cash, and I can take this to the pawn shop tomorrow, but they weren't open today. So if you want to take the necklace, I'll call it even because I know it's worth more than my debt to you."

"This is really somethin'. Where'd you get it? Did you pinch it from some old lady?"

"No, I'm a lot of things, but I'm not a thief. This has been in my family for generations." Max decided that a little enhancement could increase his perception of its value. "It was handed down to me last year. I gave it to my wife as a birthday gift, but she wants you to have it, so we can clear up our little problem, here."

"Very generous of her. Is it real?"

"Yes, yes, of course. Rubies and diamonds. See how it lights up like fire in the lights? It's very special and very, very old. Once you give it to a lady friend, or your wife of course, you'll see what I mean." Max held his breath, waiting for Bernie's response.

He could see that Bernie was taken with the jewels. They danced and tempted him as he ran his hands over them. He looked up at Max and studied his eyes. "I think you're honest, and there ain't too many of those kind around here; know what I mean? So I'll take this in exchange for the money owed. You'll be free and clear. I can't wait to give it to my girl." He winked and jabbed Max. "Not my wife – know what I mean?"

The moment he removed his hand so that Max could replace it in its wrapping, the stones went cold; Max hoped Bernie was not aware of their dimming color. He quickly packaged it up before the mob member sitting across from him had a chance to see what he had, shook hands with Bernie who was now grinning from ear to ear, tipped his hat, and left the bar. Max ran all the way home through the storm. Maisy was waiting for him when he came in; he was soaked through and through and shivering like a junkyard dog. There was no time for small talk.

"He took the necklace. The rubies went stone cold after I handed them over. There's not a minute to lose. I'll pack our bags, you go ask for the last of your pay; we have to get out of here!"

The wait at the train station seemed to last forever, but in fact, it was only twenty minutes. The fleeing couple was surprised and thrilled to find that there was an evening train leaving the station and heading to Michigan shortly. Maisy had put aside the weekly rent money already which they would not be needing now, and with her last wages from the boarding house mending jobs, they had managed to scrape up enough for the tickets.

There were just a few other passengers waiting in the car with them, but the train had to stay on schedule and would not leave until the very second it was supposed to. Max jiggled his leg nervously, as Maisy twisted her handkerchief tightly until it looked more like a straw than a lady's fancy cloth.

Leaning over and whispering in her husband's ear, Maisy asked, "What happened? Can you tell me now?"

"Let's just say that he took the necklace because it was glowing so strongly, it practically danced out of my hands, but I saw that the moment that my hand disconnected from it, it went cold and dull. It was as if the necklace knew what was at stake! I quickly shoved it back into the wrapper before he noticed. I'm afraid once he takes it out to look at it again, he won't be too impressed. Maisy, I never realized before how attached to us the jewels are. We never had to worry about them being stolen, because we seem to be the only ones they reveal their beauty to."

"My, it's a good thing you didn't take it to a jeweler or pawn shop. They would have told you it has no value."

"Yes, well, I'm afraid that's just what Bernie will do, and I don't want to be around when he discovers the truth."

Maisy asked with a thoughtful frown, "Max, do you realize the necklace saved your life and possibly mine? Do you think it sacrificed itself for us?"

"I'm beyond trying to figure it out. But it just hit me, that we -- oh, good we're moving."

They both breathed a sigh of relief. "What were you going to say?"

"Nothing, let's just be happy to be on our way." Max laughed as he sought the comfort of her hand. "Well, that's one way to get you home to visit your mother." They sighed with relief and kissed each other quickly before settling in for the trip through West Michigan which would eventually stop at the Muskegon Depot. Max tightened his hold on Maisy's hand. "I love you, Maisy Woods."

"I love you, Max Woods." Maisy sounded light-hearted, but she still worried whether Bernie would come looking for them someday.

What they would never know, is that Bernie discovered that his girlfriend, the intended recipient of the necklace, had been cheating on him with his best friend. After a good beating, she was lucky to escape with her life. His friend didn't. The necklace was tossed in his dresser drawer, later to be found by his wife, who assumed it was for her. She held it up to the light and declared it too gaudy to wear. She threw it in her jewelry box where it stayed for the next month or so when she gave it to the cleaning lady as a bonus for doing a good job before her upcoming party. The cleaning lady quickly pawned it for money to feed her kids. It remained in the pawn shop on display in the case, dull and lifeless, for the next ten years, and when it was finally sold as a cheap trinket, it once again began to travel from hand to hand seeking its rightful owner.

Chapter Fourteen

As the train rounded the base of Lake Michigan and began heading north, the runaway couple caught the brilliant colors of the sunrise, bringing with it a promise of a new day, a promise of a new start. Once they arrived at the station in Muskegon, Maisy and Max were in a dilemma about how to get home. With no money and no way to contact their family, they would have to walk along the shore of Muskegon Lake to Bluffton, approximately five and a half miles, dragging their luggage with them. But then Max remembered that the ice and coal company he had worked for was just up the street next to the train tracks. They walked that far and begged a ride from an old friend who was just getting ready to leave on his route towards their home. Maisy's mother was more than surprised when her delivery of coal also brought her daughter and son-in-law. It had only been ten months since the young couple had left home, but to mother and daughter it had been an eternity. The reunion was sweet, but even more so when they sent a neighbor boy to run down the block to get Edward and Lena. Edward had missed Max terribly – Lena not so much. But with the families all back together, they made plans for a picnic. Max and Maisy agreed to live with her mother as long as she would let them help out with anything she needed. Max promised to work on repair and maintenance that had been let go for too long, and Maisy would help with the cooking, as well as get right back into the alterations and sewing she had always done with her mother.

For a time Max did not have a drop to drink, and he even stayed away from cards completely. He returned to his former job with the coal and ice company, and brought money home to help with expenses. Everything was wonderful and Maisy was so happy. But in June, when he was around the vaudevillians, heard stories of their travels, and saw how successful Buster was becoming, he began to be jealous. He had never intended to be a regular laborer for the rest of his life. He had dreamed of fame and the spotlight since he was a kid. He still held on to his plans of improving his act and traveling on tour; he couldn't let that idea go. And when the vaudevillians left in August, as they usually did, and Max and Maisy were not on the train with them, he began to feel despair. The fall seemed lonely without his summer friends, and eventually he began to go to the pub for a nice game of cards. At least, he didn't gamble this time, he just played cards. Then one day, in November, Maisy said she needed to talk to him, and everything changed.

Maisy called him into their bedroom where they could have some privacy. Max had no expectations of anything other than talk, because without the necklace they were the same as any other married couple, coming together when their needs arose. They were still young so the lovemaking could be vigorous at times, but it would never be like it had been with the rubies, and he knew it. So when he entered the bedroom, he was surprised to find Maisy sitting on the bed with a grin.

"Maisy, my love, in the middle of the day?"

"No, silly, I didn't call you here for your favorite activity. I have something to say. Max, come here, sit, please." She patted the bed next to her. "I have some exciting news."

He did what she asked, now very curious, and being a man, also completely blind to the obvious. "What is so important that you have to call me in here on a Saturday afternoon? I have work to get done before winter."

"Honey, I've been waiting a while so I was sure, but I can tell you now." Maisy took a deep breath, pulled Max's hand to her abdomen, and said, "You are going to be a father."

There was silence as Max tried to comprehend what she was saying, but once her words were processed, he was overcome with joy. "Maisy, my darling, how long have you known?"

"I suspected it last month, when I was so ill with the vomiting. We haven't been, you know, we haven't – well, without the necklace we don't do that so much anymore."

Max felt guilty with her last remark, but decided to ignore it for the moment. "Oh, Maisy, I'm so happy. A family all of our own! You've made me so happy. I promise to be the best father possible. We'll have a son, and I'll teach him to juggle. He can be a part of my act. We'll be a team like The Keatons. Maybe we can join the circus and follow in my parents' footsteps."

"Whoa, whoa, take it easy," chuckled Maisy. "It might be a girl, and besides I'm done with the circus and vaudeville dreams. I thought you were, too."

"Yes, I guess I am," said Max slowly, as it hit him that he now had responsibilities beyond Maisy. A child would put a damper on traveling, and there would be a constant worry about having enough money to support and feed a baby. Even though he was thrilled with the idea of becoming a father, he knew right then and there, that his dreams of getting on the stage were over. Maisy overlooked his worried expression, because she was more than excited about becoming a mother. She was sure Max would do the right thing and take good care of them forever.

Max tucked a stray blonde hair behind Maisy's ear. "When?" he simply asked.

"June, next summer. Are you disappointed that you won't be able to go back to Chicago?"

"Not at all. We can never go there again. But I admit I had plans to follow Buster wherever his family went. I can see that won't work now. Oh well, maybe the year after that."

"Yes, maybe the year after that," but Maisy was just placating him. She never intended to go on the road again. It was too dangerous, and she had never fit in, anyway. She wanted to stay here for the rest of her life and raise her daughter near family.

≈

As the winter and cold raged on, and Maisy grew larger with child, Max continued to work delivering coal, but he hated every minute of it. His only respite was his evenings at the pub with the guys. He had been able to avoid seeing Earl to this point, except in passing, but once the colder days of the season set in, Earl began to appear at the bar for a beer and a game of cards, also. Max stayed away from him and his friends; they were too rowdy, and drank heavily. Earl often came in with his older brother, Duane, who was a well-known trouble maker and had been since he was a kid. Max was content to just have a beer or two and have fun throwing darts with the guys. Maisy was content to stay home with her ailing mother and nest. She knitted buntings and booties and sewed a wardrobe fit for a little prince- or princess-to-be.

Whenever Earl saw Maisy he was coolly polite, but as he began to notice her roundness, he secretly fumed. It was obvious that the woman he had always wanted not only belonged to another man, but would now bear that man's child. When he was alone in his bed, his thoughts swirled in the darkness of the night, and he was tortured with the image of how the child had been conceived.

Winter turned into spring and then into summer, following the same unending cycle that had been happening since the beginning of time, and along with the new season the vaudevillians returned once again. It was now June of 1915.

Maisy was excitedly anticipating the birth of her first child. Max was nervously wondering how they would be able to handle it. Maisy's mother was getting weaker, as her cough would not go away, but she would be able to help out with the baby while Maisy did the sewing. Max's biggest concern was if he could afford to financially take care of all four of them. Money was in short supply now, but even so, he always found a little to go to the pub and have a drink or two.

One night in early June, June 10th to be exact, Max had been winning at darts, game after game, the bet always being for a glass of beer. He meant to go home early, but the beers kept coming. His buddies were having fun side-betting on his games, so he stayed much longer than he anticipated. Around three in the morning, Max's step-brother came running in to tell him that Maisy was giving birth. It had happened all so quickly, but the midwife was with her now, he said. Max grabbed his flat cap and flew out of the pub with lightning speed, running unsteadily all the way home, and praying that his Maisy would be all right. Upon entering his house, he heard a child wailing. It was a strong cry. He grinned once he heard that his son had a good pair of lungs; he would grow up to be strong and healthy. When the midwife emerged from the bedroom that held his wife and child, she smiled broadly at him, and said, "Mr. Woods, it's a wonderful day! Your wife is fine, and, congratulation, you have a baby girl."

"A daughter? But that can't be. I – I -- can I see them now?"

"Sure you can. Go right in. Your missus is waiting for you."

Max's heart filled with joy when he first saw his wife with the child at her breast. He kissed Maisy's head gently and then bent down to study his newborn -- this strange creature that appeared to be from another world. "How did we get a girl, Maisy?"

Maisy laughed at Max's distress. "Oh, Max, I always warned you of the possibility. What do you think of her? Here, take her in your arms. Hold your daughter."

When Max held the little porcelain doll, he saw a carbon copy of Maisy looking back at him. She was perfection in every way – blonde hair, blue eyes, -- an angelic creation of God's. He wondered how he could have ever dreamed of having a boy. When she latched onto his little finger, and held on so tightly, he fell hopelessly in love.

Looking at Maisy in awe, he asked, "What will we name her? I had only planned for Maxwell Junior. I'm at a loss. Are you?"

"I have an idea. I hope you like it, because I have already started calling her by her new name, and it fits perfectly. I'd like to call her Ruby Clara, for the necklace and your mother."

"Ruby? It's the best name I could have ever thought of. Even though we lost what seemed to be so precious to us, we have something much better now. She'll shine just as brightly as our jewels did. And, thank you, it's an honor to name her after the mother I never knew. I'm sure my father will be so happy. I love you, my sweet Maisy, and I promise to do my very best for Ruby, always." The couple kissed happily with their bundle of joy between them. Maisy was content knowing that everything would be all right now.

It wasn't long before word spread among the residents of Bluffton about the new arrival. Visitors bearing gifts came to the house to welcome the baby girl, named Ruby, to the community. Edward was over the moon to be a grandfather, but in her natural coldness, Lena did not show much emotion. Edward broke down and cried when he heard the name of Ruby Clara, the significance of both names was not lost on him. Lena huffed when she heard the name of Clara, because even though she held no special affection for

Edward, she had always been jealous of the love that the previous wife had had with her husband.

For a time, Max barely drank at all. He went to the pub to celebrate the birth, and many mugs were purchased for him, which he felt obligated to consume, but after that one time, he stopped going. He wanted nothing but the best for his Ruby, and that meant finding some sort of work that would provide a larger income.

A few days after Ruby's birth, Buster came home. Buster was thrilled to hear that Max was a father now. He had always felt badly that he had encouraged Max to follow him to Chicago to join the vaudeville tour. The two old friends sat on the end of the dock with fishing poles in hand and talked about Buster's latest gigs, how his family was doing, and what was up next for him. When Max heard about the mishaps, which Buster could make hilariously funny, and the standing ovations, which Buster played down, Max could relive the vaudeville life through him. The visions of fame he once had danced in his head; he could see himself on stage to cheers and applause. But when he went home reality set in, and he knew it was never to be for him. Those dreams had to be put to bed once and for all.

All through the summer, Max was a good and doting father. He went to work on time and brought back a full paycheck with no stops at the bar along the way. He was determined to be the best man he possibly could. But once again, when the summer ended and the actors left Bluffton without him, he realized he had been holding out a secret hope that Maisy would agree to go back to Chicago. He had tried once to bring up the idea, and it ended in a huge fight. She would not budge. She yelled at him, saying if he wanted to go, then he should go, but she was staying. Her mother needed her, she said. And then she pleaded that Ruby needed *him*. And finally he agreed, and even felt childish for wanting something for himself when he was a family man now.

When winter arrived the dark days brought on Max's despair, and he began to go to the pub again. Late one night he was called home, when he was informed that Edward had passed away in his sleep. Losing his father, put Max in a tailspin. He had not even thought of the possibility of life without him. Max and Edward had always been close, even though his step-mother had tried to interfere with their relationship on a few occasions. After losing his mother at infancy, and now with no father to ground him, Max felt lost and alone, which was the farthest thing from the truth. While mourning his loss, the drinking escalated once again.

"Max, please don't go out tonight," begged Maisy in December. "Mama's not doing well, she's so weak, and Ruby's teething. I need some help. I need some sleep. I've been sewing all day long, and I can hardly keep my eyes open."

"Look, you're the mother. That's what women do. They walk the floor with the baby. That's not a father's job. I bring home the paycheck. I work hard all day shoveling heavy coal, breathing in all of that coal dust, getting filthy as a pig, just so you can eat. What do you want of me?"

"How dare you?" yelled Maisy. "It's not like I'm not contributing. I sew until my fingers are bloody, and without Mama's help I wouldn't even be able to do that. She has provided us with a free place to live, without one complaint. It's the least you can do to help out."

"Well, not tonight! I already have plans to go out."

"When will you be home?"

"When I get here!" Max walked out and slammed the door.

How Maisy longed for the ruby necklace so she could smooth things over by tempting him with sex. Life was more difficult than she had planned, and the ruby necklace was no more. If it had been in their possession, and she had been able to change his mind about going to the pub with a promise of sexual pleasure, what came next might not have happened.

Chapter Fifteen

On this particular night in dark December, while the snow was silently falling in large flakes sometimes called goose feathers, the men inside the pub were deeply engrossed in a game of poker. Max had decided to join in this time instead of playing darts. It began as the usual friendly game with the regulars, all of Max's drinking buddies. Max won hand after hand, thrilled with his take. He needed to prove to Maisy that what he had been doing here, at all hours, was worth it. He looked at the stash in front of him and made a somewhat sober decision to quit while he was ahead.

One of his friends said, "I'm tapped out; that's all for me."

The chair scraped on the floor as he pushed it back to go, and then someone else said "I'll take that spot, if you don't mind."

Max glanced up to see that Earl was already pulling the chair out from the table and getting comfortable.

"I don't think that's a good idea," said Max. "And besides, I'm done, too, so you'd need another to fill my spot."

"Well, that problem is solved," said a voice from behind. A heavy hand pushed Max back into his chair. "Give us a chance to win the pile you got settin' there."

Max turned to see who was talking, and was surprised to see Earl's brother, Duane, not someone he would care to see at any time let alone after Duane had been drinking and Max had a sizable amount of money in front of him. In order to avoid a ruckus, he responded, "Okay, but just one hand. I have to get home to the missus and kid."

Unfortunately for Max, his winning streak held. Normally, he would be thrilled to have bested the

Schaeffer brothers, but he knew without a doubt, that taking their money was not going to be good. Other men were standing around the table, and to leave his winnings behind would be a disgrace, it just wasn't done. So he pulled the bills towards him, stuffing the money in his pocket, as the two brothers glared. Suddenly, Duane accused Max of cheating. "There's no way anyone like you could win that much money in one night. You slipped a card up your sleeve. I saw it!"

One of Max's friends who had been standing behind him said, "That's a lie. Max did no such thing." One of the Schaeffers' friends pushed him, then a punch was thrown, and before Max saw it coming, he was clocked square on the jaw. It didn't take much to take him down, with the help of the liquor, which had already caused him an unsteady stance. Hearing nothing but a roar in his ears, he was, more or less, passed out on the floor while the fight raged above him. Fists landed heavily, breaking noses and splitting lips, as each side defended their friend and relative. Somehow through it all, Max was able to sit up and drag himself off to the side. He used the only table that was left as support to pull himself up, and then while then sound of flesh on flesh smacked behind him, he staggered out the back door.

The world outside was white on white. The street was deep with snow. There was no difference between sky and ground, and for the drunk that was weaving down the street, it was almost impossible to tell which way was up. He took one step after another in the general direction of home, or so he thought. Whether he had a concussion from the punch, or whether the alcohol had finally caught up with him, or both, he suddenly stopped in the middle of the road, not knowing which way to turn. He was lost in his own home town. The next decision he made was the worst one possible. He chose to go down an alley which he believed led him to his back door, but was in fact, the back of the bar. He had made a complete circle.

The next thing he knew he was being jostled by a police officer.

"Max! Max Woods, wake up. Get up, now, tell me what happened."

When he opened his eyes he saw people standing above him, and he heard Earl yelling, "Let me at him, the lowlife scum! I'll kill him."

Another cop was holding Earl, while Max watched in a daze. "What happened? Where am I?"

"You killed my brother!" screamed Earl.

"What? Duane, you mean?"

"What do you have to say for yourself, Max?" asked the cop who was also his neighbor.

It was then that Max noticed the lifeless body on the ground next to him. Duane looked like he was sleeping in a pile of white powder, as the snow had continued to fall and cover him like a blanket. "I don't know what you're talking about. I'm not even sure how I got here," he mumbled, rubbing his eyes to clear his vision.

Earl yelled, "I saw it all. My brother confronted him about cheating, and Max took a swing at him. Duane hit his head on that rock that's used as a doorstop for the kitchen. He's dead! He's dead! How could you?" Earl was crying. There was no doubt his pain and anguish was real. And because everyone in the bar knew the reason the fight had broken out in the first place, it all made sense. What they didn't know was that Earl and Duane had followed Max out, intending to rob him. It was Duane's idea, but Earl always went along with what his big brother said. When they found Max passed out, they laughed at the easy pickings, but when Duane began to put all of the money in his own pocket, leaving Earl out of the cut, their own fight broke out, which was not unusual for the brothers. They began to scuffle, first with a head lock and then a few blows landing to the body. It was Earl who had actually thrown the deadly punch at his brother. It was Earl who had killed him. And as soon as he realized his brother's limp body was not going to respond, he ran inside the bar, yelling that Max had killed Duane.

There wasn't a soul who doubted otherwise. Max was taken away in cuffs, and Maisy was left at home wondering where her husband was. When someone from the bar, came to tell her what had happened, she couldn't believe it. It was impossible; Max was never violent. Max in jail? She didn't have a clue what to do. Her mother was sick and she had an infant at home; she couldn't leave, so she paced the floor and waited until morning. In the light of day she went next door and asked a neighbor what she should do. She found someone to take care of her child and another neighbor drove her to the jail. She was allowed a few minutes to talk to Max, but most of the time there was no talking, he just hung his head in shame. Since he had been passed out at the time, he truly thought he had done it. Maisy held his hand and cried, wondering what was to become of them all.

There was no money for an attorney, and there was no bail for murder. With an eyewitness to the fight itself and others telling about how the bar fight had started, it was obvious to the authorities that what Earl said was true. The trial, which had been scheduled for the following week, was short, and the jury came back early with a verdict. While some thought that justice was done when Max was pronounced guilty as charged for manslaughter, others cried 'fowl'. But there was no recourse for the poor. Max was sentenced to twenty years without parole.

≈

For a while Maisy visited Max regularly, while he was at the local jail, but once the trial was over and he was moved to the state penitentiary, she had no way to get to him. She wrote letters weekly, but he never responded. He was in the deepest depression he had ever been in in his life. He chastised himself regularly, muttering, "What was I thinking? I have an infant at home who needs me. I have a beautiful wife who needs me. I've thrown it all away for the love of the drink."

Try as he might, he could never recall the complete events of that night. When he finally wrote to Maisy, it was with words he had never thought he would say. When he sealed the letter, and handed it to the guard, he sobbed like he had not done since he was a young child.

When Maisy retrieved the mail from the box, she was overjoyed to see Max's handwriting. She couldn't wait to get inside the house to read it, so she tore open the envelope and read it right there on the steps to the porch. The words were not what she expected at all; her world had just come to an end.

Dear Maisy, my wonderful wife,

I hope all is well with you and little Ruby. I pray for you daily. I have disappointed you so, and I'm not even sure how it happened. I can never face you again. Ruby will always have to live with the fact that her father is a jailbird, and worse, a murderer. I'm so glad my father is no longer with us. I would not want him to see what has become of me.

I have something to say, and it's going to be very hard for you to hear, I know, but I want you to listen to me and do what I say. You see, I'm never going to get out of here, not for a long time, anyway. From now on I will have only dreams and memories of my life with you to sustain me, and that's not a lot, since we've only been married a short time, and I had barely begun my life as a father. Ruby must not spend her life telling people that her father is in prison. You should not have to answer for me every time someone asks about your husband. So I am saying something that is very difficult, but it's what I believe is the best for all.

Maisy, dear, you need to get a divorce. Yes, I know you are crying now, I can feel it, but it's the only way. You have no one to take care of you. Your mother may not last too much longer with her lung disease, and then what will you do? Sewing is not enough. And even if you do find a different job, who is left to take care of Ruby? You know Lena won't do it. She never truly felt like I was family. So Maisy, you have to leave me and remarry.

Find someone responsible, with an income, who can take care of you the way you deserve to be taken care of. I am setting you free. It will hurt terribly the day the papers arrive for my signature, but I don't want you to try to come here. It's too far and would take too much time and money. You know what I am saying is true, so please do as I say. Do it for Ruby, if not for yourself. You are young and desirable. You should have no problem finding someone else to love.

I will be waiting for your reply, and then I never want to hear from you again. Goodbye, my love, I will always cherish our nights with the rubies. You will be in my heart forever. You are the love of my life.

I'll love you 'til the end of time, Max

Maisy sat on the front porch in full view of all to see with the crumpled letter in her lap and her head bent forward in her hands, sobbing until there were no more tears left. Then she slowly stood up and walked inside to her sleeping infant.

Chapter Sixteen

Life was very hard for a single mother in 1916. There was no government assistance of any kind. A person had to find their own way through their troubles; most in need depended on family. But if your only living relative was an ailing mother, and you had a small child to care for, and you had lost the income your husband had provided, there was nowhere to go for help. Throughout that year neighbors and friends helped Maisy the best they could. The local church would often send boxes of food, and once in a while Maisy found a charity box of needed baby items and clothing at her door. She was humiliated and embarrassed at her station in life. Sometimes she wondered what had become of them. How had Max chosen the wrong path to take? When they first married they were young and full of dreams, and now their dreams were the farthest thing from reality.

In August when Maisy turned twenty-one years old, she felt and looked haggard and run-down. Her mother had passed away a few months earlier, leaving her completely alone except for the baby. Ruby was a joy, a perfect baby in fact, but Maisy worried for her health. She could barely keep food on the table. Luckily, she was still nursing the child but if she didn't keep her own strength up, she would dry up and lose Ruby's only sustenance. With not enough sleep and too many work hours, Maisy's appearance began to deteriorate. She had dark circles under her eyes, her hair had lost its luster, and she was thin and depressed. Every day seemed more miserable than the last.

Maisy knew there was one way a woman could get money, and it was something she never thought she would ever consider, but she was desperate. One evening, she put on her best dress, fixed her hair, and applied her lipstick darker than normal. When she was in Chicago, one of the women in the boardinghouse had given her a cigarette holder. Maisy had admired it and had wondered what it would feel like to hold it like the high society women did. Although she rarely smoked, she had given it a try when the ladies of the house would sit around together. Many of them smoked while they gossiped. The vaudevillian women thought nothing of it. Maisy looked at herself in the mirror. With her heavy makeup, the cigarette holder, and wearing the last fancy dress she owned, she looked exactly like all of the women in the red light district downtown – thin and tired, but trying her hardest to appeal to what a man wanted. She studied herself from all angles. If she did this, and the neighborhood found out, she would be run out of town, and then what would happen to Ruby? Tears filled her eyes at the thought of what she was contemplating. But what was she to do? For Ruby, she would do whatever was necessary, and if it meant selling herself, she would -- but not tonight. As the tears rolled down her face, smearing her makeup as they went, she took off the dress, wiped her mouth clean, and put her everyday frock back on, covering it with an apron.

Maisy was tying the apron at her back when she answered a knock at the door. She was shocked to see Earl standing there, looking quite nervous. He was neatly combed and shaven. His hair slicked down with a center part. Maisy took a step back; she wasn't quite sure how she felt about Earl. They had avoided each other ever since Max had gone to prison for killing his brother.

Earl knew Maisy would be surprised to see him, but he was more surprised to see *her*. She barely looked like the girl he had grown up with. His heart broke to see her in such a disheveled state. "Hello, Maisy. How are you?"

"I'm doing as well as can be expected, Earl. What brings you by?"

"May I come in? I'd like to talk to you, but not in view of passersby."

"Sure – I suppose it will be okay. Come in, but please keep your voice down. Ruby's sleeping."

"Of course, of course." Earl awkwardly stepped into the dark and gloomy room. It was early evening and there should have been a light on, but Maisy did not use the electric lights unless necessary. The monthly bill was more than she was able to afford. She walked over to a kerosene lantern and lit that instead. As she did so, Earl studied her thoughtfully. The way her dress hung on her thin frame shocked him, but he was so in love with her still that she looked as beautiful to him as she had when they were teens. The glow of the lamp was more flattering than the hanging lightbulb would have been, and Earl's heart melted with sympathy and compassion.

"Please sit, Earl. Can I get you something? Coffee, perhaps? Or tea?"

"No, thank you." Maisy breathed a sigh of relief. She didn't have any coffee; it was a luxury now.

"Look, Maisy, I just came by because I heard about your mother. I want you to know how sorry I am. I know I have never expressed any kind of sympathy for your situation since Max went away. I'm sorry for that, and ashamed of myself."

"Thank you for your expressions of consolation about my mother. I appreciate it, but as far as Max, it should be I who should be ashamed. I never talked to you about your brother Duane. I'm sorry for Max's actions."

Earl was uncomfortable now, because he was the only person on Earth who knew the truth of what happened that night. At the time all he could think about was saving his own hide, and taking care of Max at the same time. Pointing the finger at Max seemed the only logical thing to do. "I understand, I really do. There was so much going on at the time, with the trial and all. I'm really sorry for testifying against him, but I had to tell the truth."

"Yes, I know, but I still can't believe he did it. It's just not like him. He was a big drinker, but I never saw anger in him when he was drunk. If anything, he was usually happier than normal. It's a puzzle to me, and

his decision that night turned my life upside down --
Ruby's too."

"How is she doing, by the way?" Earl was pleased
that Maisy was not rejecting him. When he first
knocked at her door, he wasn't sure if she would even
agree to see him, but maybe time had healed the
wounds of that horrible night.

"Ruby is wonderful; we're doing just fine."

"I wanted to stop by and tell you, that if there is
anything you need, anything at all, I want you to come
to me. I know your situation, and I would love to help
in some way, if I can. All you have to do is ask, and I
will be right there for you. Anything at all."

"Thank you, Earl. That is so kind. Buster stopped
by a time or two this summer and right before he left he
gave me some money. He insisted I take it, so we're
okay for a while."

"That was very nice of him. He was always
generous in that way."

"Yes, yes he was."

"Well, I'd better get going. It was nice to see you again."

"Yes, thank you for coming by."

At the door, Earl turned to look at Maisy. He made a decision right on the spot, knowing her answer could change the course of both of their lives. "Maisy, uh, -- may I, uh -- may I call on you again sometime soon?"

Maisy studied Earl. He was the same Earl he had always been when he followed her and Max around, uncomfortable in his own skin, never quite fitting in. But as far as she knew, he never got into any kind of trouble with the law, and there were no reports of him drinking or gambling too much. In fact after his brother died, folks said they never saw him at the bar again. She wondered what Max would think? What would he tell her to say? And then it hit her full force that he was not here to give her advice. He had given up that privilege when he had killed a man.

"Yes, Earl, you may call again. It was nice to see you, too."

Earl broke out in a grin for just a second, nodded his head, and then soberly turned to leave. He had never truly thought she would agree.

≈

Over the fall and winter, Earl would stop by to check on Maisy. She was cool in her demeanor but polite. She still was not sure she had made the right decision to let him back into her life, but she did need a man to help out now and then, and hiring a repairman was out of the question. Any one of her neighbors would have helped, but she had asked so much of them, and she was hesitant to continue asking. It made her feel so needy. Sometimes, Earl would arrive with meat or vegetables, and Maisy would ask him to stay to supper. When Maisy thought of what she had been about to do that night Earl first knocked on her door, she began to think of him as her savior. She felt nothing for him romantically; she actually felt guilt at using him the way she did because she knew his feelings for her. But there was no other choice, as far as she could see. If she had been in another town or community, any number of eligible men would have come calling, but Bluffton was such a small community, all the men her age or close to it were taken. Even then some of the taken ones had made an attempt to flirt and offer their services. Having Earl around was simply the safest way to go.

In the spring of 1917, Earl was expected for dinner at Maisy's house. There had been some town gossip about his appearances at her door so often. A single woman was not supposed to entertain a gentleman in her house alone, but they had been doing so all winter long, without a worry of what anyone thought.

Earl's visits were always platonic – he was a perfect gentleman. Sometimes when Ruby was awake, he would play with her on the floor. She was toddling around and beginning to try to say some words. He found her quite amusing, and she seemed to like him, too. Maisy was satisfied with their arrangement, but

Earl was beginning to view them both as his family, and was starting to be a little too possessive. She had some worries about that, but she tried to keep their relationship as friendly as possible. She might be selling herself out, but the way she was doing it was far better than the alternative.

On this particular night, Earl had arrived with flowers, saying that the spring evening was so beautiful that it made him think of her. He thought she would like them, because she needed something colorful and pretty in her life, he declared. After their meal, when Ruby was put to sleep, Earl asked if he could talk to her.

Maisy laughed, "Isn't that what we always do after our dinner?"

Earl smiled, answering, "Yes, but I have something serious to discuss."

"Okay," she said slowly. She could tell Earl was nervous. Maisy was worried, because she thought she knew what he was about to say, and wondered how she would respond. "Go ahead, I'll listen while I do the dishes."

"No, come and sit with me. You can worry about the dishes later."

Maisy did as she was asked, sitting next to him on the sofa – not too close but just enough to keep him interested in her. She needed him now; he was her sole means of support. She put on her sweetest smile, lowered her eyes, and asked. "What is it you want, Earl?"

"You know how I've been talking about starting my own business?"

"Sure, you've mentioned it several times."

"Well, I'm happy to say that I have begun to do just so. I've been studying the needs of the local communities, and wondering what I can give them that they need and don't have. I came up with an idea, and I decided to go ahead with it. With the rising use of automobiles, there is a greater need for fuel and repair. I've always been good with my hands, and I've tinkered with all kinds of motors, so I've decided to open a gas station. And, today I took the first step -- I bought some land this morning. It's right along US 131, a little ways north of here. There's already a house on it, but I think I can turn the barn into a repair garage and add some gas pumps. I might even sell tires, since they're always in demand. I've been putting money aside for several years, now, so when the opportunity came up, I grabbed it.

"Oh," blinked Maisy. This was not what she had expected at all. "US 131? How far north? Are you moving away?" She began to panic. If he left her, what would she do? First Max, then her mother, and now Earl? She had no romantic feelings towards him whatsoever, but he had become a friend. How would she survive without him?

"Well, it is a ways away, but uh -- I have something else to ask." Earl slid off of the couch and got down on one knee. Taking Maisy's hand in his, he asked, "Maisy, would you marry me? Will you come with me? I can give you a good life. I'll take care of Ruby, and maybe we can even have a family of our own."

Maisy was shocked at the intensity of his proposal. She could see that he really loved her, but she felt nothing except despair. "Before I answer, I have to tell you something."

"Whatever it is could never change my mind about how I feel about you, so please go ahead."

"I'm rather embarrassed to say that I am still a married woman. I know I told you that I wasn't married anymore, but I never actually got the divorce from Max. I guess I was hoping against hope that he would get out early. And truth be told, I didn't have any money for an attorney."

Even though he was upset to hear this news, it was nothing that Earl couldn't fix. "If you will have me, I will help you get the divorce. It shouldn't be too difficult with his situation. What do you say? Will you marry me? You know I love you and always have."

Maisy sucked in a deep breath, closed her eyes, said a short prayer, and then she waited for God to answer. When no words from above came, she said rather dully, "Yes, I'll marry you."

Earl was not stupid. He knew Maisy didn't love him, and that he would always have to compete with the memory of Max. And he knew he would forever have to deal with the guilt of accusing her husband of killing his brother, when in fact, he was the murderer. But he was ready to take Maisy as his own even if she didn't return his love. When she said yes, he was overjoyed. He pulled her hands to his lips and kissed them both as tears coursed down his face.

Maisy felt nothing.

Chapter Seventeen

In a much quicker time than Maisy would have thought possible, her marriage to Max was over. Earl put up the money in order to hire an attorney to draw up the papers, and once they had been signed by Max and returned by mail, they were filed in the court, and Maisy's previous life with the man she had loved with all of her heart had turned to dust – dead and gone forever. With nothing but a few pictures that had been taken by some of the vaudevillians, and a few hazy memories, it was as if there never was a Maisy and Max – except for one thing. Ruby. Max's daughter had his flashing eyes, and his spirit of adventure. She loved people and she was uninhibited and outgoing. She would put her arms out to be picked up and loved by anyone she took a fancy to. Even though she was still a child, Maisy could see that she had a lot of her father in her.

The ceremony took place on the very day they filed the papers. Since they were already in the courthouse, they simply moved to the Justice of the Peace's office, repeated some vows, and signed on the dotted line. It was over, final, -- Maisy had signed her life away.

In some ways she looked at it as if she had betrayed Max and their love. But then she remembered the time she had almost gone to a Madame's house to look for work of a very disreputable type. This seemed a far more respectable way to stay alive and take care of her daughter. But the next second she would be plagued with guilt. Wasn't marriage just another form of prostitution if there was no love involved? Wasn't she using a man for survival? Wouldn't she have to give of herself in payment in the same intimate way? On a day that should have been happy, Maisy felt nothing but shame.

Once they returned home and retrieved Ruby from the neighbor, once those chubby little arms were wrapped around her neck, and once that sweet head was snuggled to her chest, she knew she had done the only thing possible to save her daughter's life – and her own.

≈

The day after the ceremony, they put Maisy's mother's house up for sale. Maisy kept busy with the packing, trying not to remember the night before – the wedding night. Earl had been excited to finally have her in their marriage bed, but for Maisy it was just a chore that had to be done; it was expected of her. She never knew that she could be such a good actor. She tried to recall some of the feelings she had had when she wore the necklace with Max, but there was nothing. Since Earl knew nothing of the rubies and the heights of ecstasy to which they could bring her and Max, she was able to perform in a more simple way – and that's exactly what she thought of it as, performing. Luckily for her, he was not as enthusiastic as Max had been, so once the marriage had been consummated, he was ready to roll over and go to sleep, which suited Maisy just fine.

The house sold in record time, and soon they were packing to move to some unknown city or town next to a highway. A place Maisy had never heard of before. Maisy went through the motions, wondering what was in store for her in her new life, but at least she and Ruby were now assured of having a roof over their heads and food to eat, so she no longer questioned her decision. On June 10th, 1917, which was Ruby's second birthday, they set out by train to the station nearest to their new home. Once there, they would have to hire a car to take them the rest of the way. Their furniture and larger belongings would be delivered to them later. Maisy thought it was almost comical that they were going to run a filling station and auto repair shop when they did not even own a car themselves, but Earl had plans and he would not be deterred.

Life went on as it always did, one day at a time. There were chores for Maisy to keep up with while Earl built his dream, and in record time, it seemed, he was ready for business. It was slow at first until the new wave of automobiles discovered he was there, but it wasn't long before he built a good reputation and the money began flowing in.

After two months, Maisy discovered she was with child. The following spring she delivered a healthy baby boy, a playmate for Ruby, a child who could grow up and work in the garage with his father. Earl was ecstatic. Maisy poured all she had into her children, until one day when the Spanish Flu of 1918 came knocking on their door. The next few years were hell. When Earl lost both his wife and son, he began to drink. Life for Ruby was never the same.

Present Day — 2017

Chapter Eighteen

There was silence when Ronnie finished her narrative. Ivy barely moved, amazed with the story her new found friend had just related. Ronnie had told her something so unbelievable and shocking, that she didn't know what to think. How was it possible that these facts, previously unknown to her, had been dropped into her lap? She reached over for her glass, which had barely been touched, and took a sip of wine to steady herself.

"So, what do you think? Does this make sense to you?" asked Ronnie. The look on Ivy's face showed confusion and puzzlement; a slight frown creased her forehead as she tried to form a picture of the events. She seemed to be in another world. "Helloooo. Anybody in there?"

"Oh, sorry. I was trying to sort it all out." Ronnie had presented the story in a factual way, but as she was telling what she knew, Ivy had been converting it to a readable story in her head. She already knew without a doubt that this was her next novel.

"Ronnie, in a nutshell, here is what I heard you tell me. Maisy and Max had a child named Ruby. After Max went to prison, Maisy married Earl and moved north along US 131 where they started Schaeffer's Garage. Maisy and her son, Henry, died as a result of the Spanish Flu Epidemic."

"Yes, that's the story Max told his son, my great-grandfather, and it was then passed to my grandfather. Through photos and writings we know that part to be true. We were always interested in Max Woods because we were told he knew Buster Keaton, and therefore my interest in Bluffton and the Actor's Colony. And of course, the story of his father and mother, Edward and Clara, and their time in the circus was always fascinating."

"But what I don't get is the rest of the story about Max. When did he get out of prison, and how is it that you are a descendant?"

"From my research, I discovered he was released in 1935, when he was forty years old, and that fits with the rest of the story, which he only told after his second wife died, who is my two times great-grandmother. When he was released, the first thing he did was to go visit Maisy and his daughter. He was devastated that they were no longer living in Maisy's mother's house. He was told by neighbors who still remembered her, that Maisy had married Earl and moved away. He assumed she had remarried after all of that time he was away, but he was shocked to find out it was Earl. He talked to neighbors and learned of the gas station and auto repair business Earl had built. Max tracked him down. He just wanted to see Maisy and Ruby. When he arrived, Earl informed him that Maisy and both of the children had died in the flu epidemic. And to stab the knife in his back one more time, Earl confessed to having killed his own brother by accident. He laughed at the fact that Max had paid for Earl's own sin with twenty years of Max's life. There was a horrible fight, and Max said he would have killed Earl that night, but the threat of returning to prison again was too much to bear. He stopped himself when he realized he was pummeling Earl to death with his fists. He returned a defeated man, but eventually met and married my two times great-grandmother, a much younger woman, and they began a family. I am the offspring of son number two."

"But, this is unbelievable! I know you haven't read my book yet, but the Ruby in my book is the same person as the Ruby in your story. Ruby was raised by Earl Schaeffer. She always believed that Schaeffer was her last name. As a matter of fact this is the first I am hearing about Max. Ruby didn't die in the epidemic. Earl lied; he was a cruel alcoholic. Ruby had a horribly rough life until she was fifteen. But the amazing part is that you and I are both descended from Max; we're cousins of a number too high to count – for me anyway

– maybe fourth or fifth cousins. Anyway, through Max, we share the same blood line."

"Are you kidding me? I knew there was something familiar about you. There must be a family resemblance I'm picking up on. Do you suppose that Gina woman knew, too?"

"I'm beyond trying to figure that one out. But you really have to read the story about Ruby and Sal, because the legacy of the necklace continues in a way neither one of us could ever have imagined, and I'm not even sure if we'll ever be able sort it out, completely. I'm truly blown away! I wish Ruby were still alive to hear this. She never got along with Earl, and now I understand why. He probably resented her because she lived and Maisy and his son didn't."

"Do you mean the necklace was real? We always thought it was a fanciful tale, told by an old man to make his life larger than it actually was."

"Oh, no, it was real, all right. That's it on Maisy's neck in your photo. By some strange coincidence it came into Sal's hands and he gave it to Ruby. Sal said that Al Capone gave it to him; we might never know how it came to be in Capone's possession."

Ronnie sat up straight. "Where is it? Do you know?"

"Sadly, it disappeared once again. Ruby had it until the 1930s, but lost it when Sal died. She was hoping I could find it in her home, but I couldn't."

"You were able to talk to Ruby about it?" Ronnie was truly shocked at this turn of events.

"Yes, my great-grandmother lived to be 102 years old. I knew her well, and I loved her so much. As a matter of fact, she gave me permission to interview her so that I could tell her story. All of the facts in my book are true; I just embellished a bit. Well, maybe more than a bit, but it made for a good novel."

"Well, I can't wait to get home and read it! And speaking of which, it's much later than I thought. I'd better get going before my mother loses her patience with the kids."

Ronnie stood up and carried her glass to the sink. The young women studied each other and then broke out laughing. They were cousins – of a sort, genealogically, that is, but with a lot more in common than just that. Ivy had gone to the film festival to learn about Buster Keaton thinking he would be the subject of her next project, and in fact, he would only have a small role in the story. But Buster had brought the two of them together – or had he? Maybe Gina would have found a way to put them together no matter what.

"Cousin," said Ivy, as she hugged Ronnie goodbye.

"Cousin. I'll contact you as soon as I finish reading about Ruby. I think it's going to be a long night, because I know I won't be able to put it down until the end. I have a feeling there's even more to this than we know."

Chapter Nineteen

With the click of the door, Ivy closed Ronnie's story on Maisy and Max. Ronnie was the one who had known that chapter of the ruby and diamond necklace, something neither Ruby nor Ivy had ever thought to question before tonight. In return, Ivy had been able to add more to Ruby's story, which had been previously unknown to Max's descendants. The next thing to do was to make a chart of events and to do a basic family tree so she could see it on paper. It always helped to have a visual. She could barely wait to get started, but as she was putting the last of the dishes in the dishwasher, she heard her little guy cooing in the next room. He always woke up so happy. What a treasure he was.

Ivy wiped the soapy water off of her hands and went to see her son. He was on his back kicking his legs and waving his arms in a flurry. He loved to make the bed bounce.

Instead of baby talk, Ivy always reverted to her Michigander accent, when talking to Buddy. Dropping g's was comfortable for her, and seemed to soothe him. "Hey, Buddy. What cha doin'? Hmmm? Are you ready for somethin' ta eat? Oh, oh. I think I'll need ta change a diaper first. Can you hold on for a bit? Mommy will be real quick. There ya go. How's that? Feelin' better?"

Before Buddy came along, Ivy could not imagine taking care of an infant by herself, or talking to someone who couldn't answer back. She had done some babysitting when she was young, but not enough and definitely not for an infant. With Nancy's help, they had poured through many books and magazines to learn the basics, and to figure out what kind of furniture and other items were required. Shopping had been the fun part, but once Buddy was born, reality had set in. She was alone. Yes, Nancy was next door, and even Matt walked the floor with Buddy once in a while, but it was not the same as having a husband to share the duties with.

Nancy was pleased that her man had a chance to see what having a baby in the house could be like, and Matt was crazy about Buddy. They seemed to have a special bond. Even though Nancy ached for a baby of her own, month after month there was no evidence of pregnancy. Ivy felt terribly sorry for her. Here she was a married woman wanting a child with every fiber in her being, and Ivy, accidentally and without having a husband, had discovered herself to be pregnant. It had been difficult to break the news to Nancy, but Nancy was who she was – kind, generous, and compassionate. She never once showed any jealousy, but instead kept saying, 'my day will come. I believe God has plans for me.' And indeed he did, because right before Ivy was to leave for the Buster Keaton Film Festival, Nancy announced that she was expecting a child. The two friends were thrilled that they would have babies close in age. Now it was Ivy's turn to support Nancy through the long months to come.

"Okay, baby, let's get you something to eat, and then you can sit in your bouncy chair. Would you like that?"

Ivy felt a bumping and nudging on her leg. "Oh, Percy, I almost forgot about you." The Siamese meowed and licked his lips. "You're hungry, too? My, I have been neglectful, haven't I? Let me put Buddy down first, and then I'll get you something. And once I get you guys settled, Mommy's going to do some research."

As Buddy sat in his seat waving his fat arms around to make the up and down movement he seemed to adore, and Percy cleaned himself from head to toe while curled up on the magazines on the coffee table, Ivy began to make notes on her laptop. She was really curious about Max and Maisy. She wondered how Max had taken the news after he learned Maisy had married Earl. And she wondered how things would have been different if Maisy had not died, or Ruby had not left the gas station to go with Sal. How sad that Ruby was living in Whitehall in 1935, a single woman with a child of her own to raise – Ivy's very own grandmother, Olivia, and all the while, her true father had been seeking her out. After Sal's death in 1933, Ruby had moved into town leaving her cottage on the lake for summer getaways only. She eventually married a pastor, and even though they kept the cottage, they never lived in it permanently. After several generations had passed, Ruby had willed it to Ivy, but the house had to be forfeited to the State through an auction as a form of reimbursement for Ruby's Medicaid Recovery. Ivy had not been in the cottage since Fox, who she had been seeing at the time, had won the bid on *her* house. It was a sore spot that would never heal, until Ivy was willing to forgive and forget.

Ivy wondered how things would have been for Ruby had she known that Earl was not her father. Maybe she would have taken a stand at an earlier age and found a way to get out of that dysfunctional household. But if that had happened maybe she would not have met Sal, who was working for Al Capone at the time. If Ruby and Sal had never met and married, the family tree would be fractured, and then Ivy, and even Buddy, would not be here.

Rubbing her head in wonder, she thought how complicated life could be. She had been guilty just like everyone else of making fun of soap operas and bizarre movie plots, but life had just provided the craziest plot of all.

She closed her laptop with an unsatisfying click. She would most likely never solve the rest of this mystery. The elusive necklace was gone forever – and what would she do with it anyway, without a man to love? Isn't that what it was for? To bring two lovers together in a way that would never tear them apart? Maisy and Max had lost that bond the moment he had sold the necklace to pay his debt. Their close bond had deteriorated the moment they were separated from it. Although Maisy always loved him, Max had lost his way, and because of it, a whole chain of events had occurred that were most likely never meant to happen. But then why did the necklace surface again? And why in Sal's possession only to have him die on the porch of the cabin with the necklace now nowhere to be found?

"Well, sweetness," she said, glancing down at her son, "I guess some questions are not meant to be answered. But your mother has a very creative mind, and I can make one heck of a story out of this. I can't wait to get started! Look out publisher. Here I come!"

Chapter Twenty

The sun went down with the love stories of Edward and Clara, Maisy and Max, and Ruby and Sal swirling in Ivy's head. She couldn't seemed to stop the lovers from popping into her thoughts. It was as if she were wired on the caffeine of the largest cup of café au lait the French had to offer, or a triple espresso Italian-style, both in true Gilmore Girls fashion. With Buddy down for the night and her eyes beginning to burn from the long and exhausting day, Ivy was finally able to lay her head on her pillow. Percy curled up next to her and began the grooming process once again – he was possibly the cleanest cat in the world. His gentle licking lulled her; once in a while his rough dry tongue would take a swipe or two at her forearm as if it were an extension of his own body. His grooming habits had a calming effect, and she finally succumbed to the darkness and the haunting dreams that were to follow.

Images of a man who loved her beyond reason, someone who would lay down his life for her, someone who would sacrifice everything to protect her filled her head. She floated on fanciful thoughts of handsome men with dark hair, flashing eyes, and sex appeal that would make any girl swoon. One in particular had broad shoulders, a firm flat chest, and strong arms. Was it Edward? Was it Max? Was it Sal? She couldn't see him clearly. Each face morphed into another, until she recognized one particular person. 'Fox,' she cried in her sleep. 'Where have you been? Come for me. I need you. I want you. I miss you so. Come –

Ivy woke up with a start to discover that her arms were outstretched, reaching for him, aching for his touch, wanting his body next to hers – and then she heard her son cry. She sat up with a fuzzy head, not sure where she was at first. By the time she got her bearings and got up to check on him, he was already back to sleep. She stood in the darkness of her cold living room, looking out at the crescent moon, its filmy cloud-covered sliver mocking her with its incompleteness. Like the moon she, too, felt incomplete and lonely. Ivy covered her eyes with her hands and sobbed.

Mornings were different now. His Highness and Lord of the Manor, Buddy von Morton, demanded a change of his royal diaper, with a meal immediately following produced from the purest goat's milk which had been warmed to perfection. He required quality time only from his royal servant and mother, the Queen of Wabaningo. "Oh, my son, what wouldst I ever have done without thee?" It was a game Ivy played with Buddy every morning. It allowed Ivy to have a sense of humor over the loss of her free time. She was grateful to Ruby for the money she found in the cottage garage, because after the baby was born, she had been able to quit her job and focus on him, and spend every free moment writing. Now that royalty checks were coming in, she was barely tapping into the gold and silver certificates she had unearthed at the cottage on White Lake. But there were plenty left, so His Majesty would have a healthy college fund, as long as his mother, the Queen, lived a simple peasant life.

Once Buddy was settled in his colorful play yard, which was placed in her living room next to her desk, she could open her computer. As he cooed at the mobile slowly moving over his head, Ivy open her genealogy account and began a search. The very first thing she wanted to look up was Ruby's birth certificate. In only a matter of seconds, she had it pulled up. Why had she never done this before? The father's name was stated clearly – Maxwell Jeremiah Woods. If only Ivy had thought to do a family tree for Ruby, but she had just gone on Ruby's verbal story, without checking facts. Apparently, Ruby had never had a need for her birth certificate, or she would have discovered this very important fact. More than likely, if she had looked for one, she would have looked in the wrong county and thought that none existed. Without computers, it would have been an impossible search. So many babies were born at home then, and records were not as important as they were now, and the Social Security system, which required proof of birth before applying for an SSN had not yet been put into place. And she certainly would not have needed one to attend school.

Next, she looked up Max's death record. Ivy was shocked to find that he died at the age of 100 in 1995. He had lived in Muskegon his whole life. A quick calculation told her that Ruby was 80 at that time. She had been strong and healthy then, and she was living only 30 minutes from her biological father. What if she had done her homework and then told Ruby what she had discovered while Ruby was still alive? How would she have received this news? Maybe she was better off at her age, not knowing. Ivy knew that was absurd. Was anyone ever better off not knowing who their real father was? At that thought, Ivy dropped the glass of water she had been sipping. Luckily, it was an unbreakable plastic tumbler and only water spillage had occurred on her carpet.

"Oh no! What have I done?" she cried. She was not referring to the water. She was referring to her breaking heart, and maybe to Buddy's disappointment in her, if he discovered the truth when he was older. Would he hate her when he learned about his father? Hadn't Nancy warned her – begged her, in fact, -- to be honest? Ivy stared at Ruby's birth certificate. Max Woods was a father she had never known, and someone who could have changed the course of her life. She turned to look at her precious son, her little lord who could not yet sit up alone without toppling over. She forced herself to reach into the desk drawer, and pull out a manila envelope that held her important documents. Then she slowly withdrew the one that showed the seal at the top, Muskegon County Vital Statistics. It was Buddy's birth certificate. She had struggled with the form she was required to fill out; Nancy had convinced her at the time to do the right thing. Then, after the fact, she had changed her mind, but to block it out emotionally, she had begun to call her son Buddy Morton. But there it was in black and white. With tear-filled eyes she read -- Mother: Ivy Morton. Father: Fox Marzetti. Date of Birth: April 26, 2017. Sex: Male. Name: Salvatore Fox Marzetti.

Ivy smoothed the paper and touched his name. She would never get over him, and the worst part was it was all her fault. She was stubborn and unforgiving. She had been unyielding in her beliefs that he was trying to scam her, and maybe he had been, but she realized now that people came with flaws. Max had had weaknesses which got him into terrible trouble, but no matter what, he had truly loved Maisy and Ruby. She could only imagine the heartbreak he had gone through when he discovered that both mother and daughter were lost to him forever. Wasn't it the same with Fox? Flaws or not, he was Buddy's father. She had no reason to keep him from his son. It was cruel, she saw that now. Ivy had never seen any violent tendencies in Fox. She had never seen Fox display anything but kindness and gentleness. There was no reason on Earth to keep them apart. She had been such a fool.

The tears flowed more freely as Ivy picked up her son. She pulled him in close, and stroked his soft downy head, as she whispered, "I'll make it right, baby boy. I'll make it right. I promise."

Chapter Twenty-one

The fall colors had popped on the trees. The world was brightly painted with oranges, reds, and yellows, the same colors Buddy saw daily while playing with his toys, but in nature it was amazing annual occurrence, and today, contrasted sharply with the sapphire sky. Some years, autumn was more festive than others, depending on the fickle weather. For the colors to be bright, the days had to be warm with an overnight cold snap, and it was especially enjoyable when the following day had warmed up again to summer temperatures. It was then that the experience of viewing the trees could be invigorating. The sun would warm the dying leaves and create an intoxicating smell. When Ivy opened the drapes and looked out her window, she saw tree tops and fallen leaves at the edge of the parking lot. Her face lit up at the scene before her. God's painting was waiting for her, and it was a perfect day for an outing.

"Buddy, eat up, because Mommy's taking you out today." Once her son was well-fed, bathed, and clothed, she called Nancy. Ivy was anxious to tell her all about the weekend with Ronnie and the new things about Ruby that she had learned. The phone rang and rang. It was only after it went to voice mail that she realized it was a workday for everyone else but her, and glancing at the clock she could tell Nancy had already left home. She would never answer her phone while driving, so she was most likely on the road.

"Where should we go, pumpkin?" There were so many options. She could take a ride out to the lighthouse and then walk along the channel. Or she could take a ride to the Muskegon State Park and hike there, or she could go all the way to Muskegon and revisit the Bluffton area. "Yes, that's it! We'll go to Muskegon."

She flipped open her computer once the idea hit her and the plan began to develop.

"Well, let's see, little man. Mommy has an idea. We are going to the big lake. Yay!" She raised Buddy's arms up high and watched his toothless face break out in a grin. Then she did it again, "Yay. Way up high." What a delight to teach him new things. Turning back to her computer she opened the genealogy search window, then clicked on census records. Maisy and Max were married in 1913 and he was incarcerated by 1916, so they fell between the cracks, since the census only came out every ten years, at the beginning of every decade. Ivy bit her lip while she thought of the best way to go about this. Both Maisy and Max had grown up in Bluffton, so there would be a record of them living in their parents' houses. She clicked on the 1910 census and then typed in Edward Woods. Bingo! There he was, listed as the head of household. He had a wife – Lena; a step-son; a step-daughter; and a son – Max. It was exactly what she had been looking for. She copied the address in the sidebar on Edgewater. Her next search was for Maisy Abernathy, since she didn't know Maisy's mother's first name. And with a few more clicks she was on the page she was hoping to find. Maisy's mother's name was Minnie, and Maisy, her daughter, was 15 years old. They, too, lived on Edgewater, and by the house number, only a short distance from Max. Ivy stopped a moment to think about the fact that these two people, who she had recently learned about, Maisy and Max, were her great-great-grandparents. They were long gone by the time she was born, but it would not have been too late for Ruby to have a relationship with her father. When Max was released from prison, she was only twenty years old; it was shortly after Sal's death. Max would have been able to meet his granddaughter, Ruby, if only Earl had not lied.

"So, that's it, Buddy. We're going to Muskegon to see where *your* three times great-grandparents and your four-times great grandparents, Edward and Clara, lived. And then I'm taking you to the big lake! Wheee!"

≈

The drive through Bluffton was completely different this time. Ivy was looking at it through new eyes, imagining where the docks were placed, what it must have looked like when Maisy and Max were dating. She could see in her mind more clearly now summer days when Buster would organize a ball game, or Max took Maisy out in a row boat. The house Max had grown up in had been torn down and replaced by a newer building, maybe sometime in the fifties, but Maisy's mother's house was still standing. The lilac bush was gone, most likely overgrown and removed long ago. Ivy could see in her mind's eye where Earl had caught Maisy and Max kissing while she wore the famous ruby necklace. The very thought of that necklace warmed her and made her blush. She had missed the opportunity to hold it in her hands, but Ruby's detailed description left nothing to the imagination.

The house, a small bungalow, had a plaque outside stating the year it was built – 1899. It was a small and unassuming wood-sided cottage, but most probably, the interior décor now was twenty-first century. Even though all of the houses here were old, they were still on desirable lake property and the price came high. But back then, it was just a simple lake neighborhood. She could see it all in print, now. Yes, this was perfect. She was ready to delve into her next project, and she would call it simply, 'Maisy and Max.'

Ivy glanced in her rearview mirror which she had positioned to see her son. He was happy as he always was whenever the car was moving. "Okay, Bud, let's go to the lake! What is that you say? You thought this was the lake? Oh, just wait, you ain't seen nothin', yet." Ivy worked her way through the residential streets and back out to Lakeshore Drive which would take her to Pere Marquette Park, the pride of Muskegon – the beach.

Once she rounded that curve and was able to see the full view of the water, she was happy. Lake Michigan always did that to her. It brought her peace, even with the rough water of the winter season, but today the waves were gently lapping at the shore and the sun was so warm it felt like summer. There was plenty of parking space right in front of the beach. They sat a moment and looked at the water. With no visible sign of the opposite shore, it felt like an ocean. Most first-timers were shocked.

Ivy got her son out of the car, but instead of carrying him in his car seat, she took him in her arms. She placed a safari hat on his head with an elastic band under his chin. She kissed his fat cheek – he was just too cute. Once he was out of the car, he squealed with delight at the seagulls, trying to imitate their call. Ivy laughed out loud. He was so funny. They walked a ways on the sidewalk, and then Ivy turned onto the walk that cut across the sand to the shore and the pier. She would not go out on the pier with her son, but it sure was tempting. The lighthouse was clearly visible and calling to her, but the walk would be too dangerous with an infant in her arms. When they neared the shoreline, Ivy sat in the warm sand with her son. She took off his shoes so he could feel beach sand for the first time in his life. It was such a joy to experience the world through a baby's eyes. He giggled and cooed, and then began to kick his fat little legs to make the sand fly. He was such a boy! She balanced him by holding his waist, and then she carefully removed her hands. He wobbled a few times, and then maybe because of the soft sand propping him up, he was able to sit for the first time by himself. He seemed very excited with his accomplishment. Ivy was so proud. After a few moments, she removed her own shoes, stood with Buddy and rose to go to the water's edge. She should have done this earlier, but she had thought he was too young yet. Ivy bent down to let Buddy dangle his feet in the water, just the toes, because it was still quite cold for a baby. He didn't care that it was too chilly for him, he wanted more. She dunked his feet once again, and then again. When her back began to ache, she decided he had had enough, so she began to walk back to the car. Buddy decided he wanted to be in control. He began to cry and reach for the water as she walked away. "Shhh. We're going bye-bye. Don't fuss now. Wanna go for a ride?"

As Ivy walked back toward the car, she jiggled her son and cooed to him to try to make him stop crying. With her head down, she almost walked into a couple strolling towards her. When she glanced up, she was looking at a face with deep brown Italian eyes, and a dark curl on his forehead. He was wearing his standard fedora. "Fox!"

"Ivy!" he said at the exact same time. "What are you doing here?"

For a moment she was speechless. She felt very awkward and uncomfortable seeing him with another woman. And then she remembered she was holding her son, and fear set in. "Uh, we just came to the beach to enjoy this beautiful day. How – how are you? Are you in town for work?" Ivy asked as she patted Buddy on the back.

"I'm fine, yes, just fine. Uh – oh—this is Mandy Baker. Yes, Mandy, mm hmm. Mandy, this is Ivy Morton, a – uh – a friend of mine."

"Nice to meet you," Mandy said, as she glanced at Fox and back again. She reached out to touch Buddy on the arm, but he pulled back. "What a cutie pie. Is he unhappy about something?"

Buddy had stopped crying upon seeing the new faces. He was intensely interested in Fox, staring at him as if he were a new item he had just discovered.

"Yes, he didn't want to leave the water, apparently."

Fox, turned a deep shade of red, and asked quietly, "Yours?"

Ivy shifted her eyes from Fox to Mandy and back to Fox again. "Ah, no. No. I'm – I'm – uh, babysitting." It would have been the perfect time, if he had not been with someone. He obviously had a new girlfriend. He had had his arm around her waist when they first came face to face. Ivy couldn't help herself. She let her eyes roam to his left hand. No ring. She exhaled deeply. But then she thought to herself, 'Check out *her* finger.' And there it was. A rather large diamond on the fourth finger of her left hand. Ivy almost passed out. "Well, nice seeing you. Have a fun day at the beach." She almost ran to the car, which luckily was only a few spots away.

Fox noticed the change in her pallor, and guessed she had noticed that he was engaged. Had she expected him to remain a monk? She must have known what she had done to him. He had tried calling over and over again. She had refused to talk to him. He had even found Nancy's number and contacted her, asking her to intervene, but Nancy said she could not make Ivy change her mind about him. It was the worst feeling in the world to think that someone you loved thought you were a worthless swindler, when nothing could be further from the truth. He was done pining over her. She didn't want him; that much was clear.

Mandy noticed how Fox's stance changed as Ivy walked away. His shoulders slumped, and he looked down at the ground as the woman backed her car up and drove away. Mandy took his hand in hers to comfort him for whatever had just happened. It was lifeless, and unwilling to curl around hers. Her woman's intuition told her this was trouble, and not over yet. Tonight she was going to make sure Fox remembered that they were engaged and going to be married in the spring. Tonight, he would think of no one but her.

$$\approx$$

"Did you see that ring, Buddy? It was the gaudiest thing I have ever seen. Who would want to wear something that huge? That's ridiculous. Who is this Mandy, anyway? She must have made a move on him the moment he left me! What? Oh, that's right *I* left *him*, but whatever the reason, he sure didn't wait long to commit to someone else. Yes, it has been over a year since I saw him last, but the point is – what is the point? I've lost him for good, haven't I? And worst of all, I screwed things up for you. I'm such an idiot."

Swiping away tears that threatened to hinder her driving, Ivy glanced back at Buddy to see what he thought of her ranting, but she discovered she was talking to a baby who couldn't care less, because he was out like a light. He hadn't heard a word she said, and that was probably good, because she had been talking smack about his father.

Ivy imagined another scenario where she ran into Fox at the beach; he would be alone, of course. He would ask about the child and she would tell him that she was sorry, but she had something important to say. She would tell him that Buddy was his son. He would be so happy. He would kiss the baby, and then he would take her in his arms and kiss her until her toes curled. They would go home together and live happily ever after as a family of three. "This stupid imagination of mine. Does it never quit?" Ivy pouted all the way home. 'Now what?' she thought.

Chapter Twenty-two

The apartment was clean and tidy. It still surprised Ivy each time she walked in the door. She had always been such a messy housekeeper, but true to form she had had to pick up her game as far as household duties went when her little bundle of joy came along. His dishes and bottles had to be cleaned and sterilized, the floor had be kept mopped regularly, and the laundry had to be done almost daily. She wanted to be the best mother ever. The disorganized Ivy of old had to go, and so she had trained herself to be a better version of her former self.

As she carried her son in and put him in his crib, she gazed at his angelic face and saw the spitting image of Fox. He had Fox's nose and Fox's coloring, and he was even developing a dimple in his chin. What would he think of his mother, if he knew she was a liar? It was a good thing he was so small. If she could find a way to fix this, he would never have to know that his father had missed out on the first months of his life. It would be torture if Fox wanted shared custody, because giving Buddy up for even a few hours when she left him with Nancy was agonizing at times. How could she ever let Fox take him for a weekend, if that was what a judge ordered?

Needing someone to talk to, she checked her phone to see if Nancy had called back. Instead she found a text message from Ronnie that she had missed.

Just finished Ruby and Sal. Love, love, loved it! I wish they were on my branch of the family tree. Lucky you. Let's get together soon. I had a good time hanging out with you.

Just hearing from Ronnie was enough to take Ivy's mind off of Fox for a moment. She was reminded of the book she was eager to start on now. With a last check on Buddy, she pulled the door to his room halfway closed, and then sat at her computer again to do more research. Going to her genealogy program again, she pulled up the death record for Maisy. It looked as though poor Maisy had died of tuberculosis, after a bout of the Spanish Flu, just as Ruby had told her. She was still a young woman, only in her early twenties. From the time she had married Max, when she was barely eighteen, she had had a child, her husband had gone to trial and then to prison for manslaughter, she had gotten a divorce, remarried, had born another child only to watch him die in a terrible plague, and then she had succumbed to tuberculosis, and died herself. It was almost too much to comprehend. Life was not easy in that time period. The document stated that Maisy was buried in a cemetery about an hour away from Ivy. Ivy decided that the next outing would be to visit her grave.

And then there was Max. He had hopes and dreams for his life with Maisy, and it all ended one night when Earl had decided to take his revenge out on Max for stealing the girl he loved and lie about who had killed his brother, Duane. Max went to prison for twenty years for something he never did. It was a wonder he didn't kill Earl when Earl confessed to him. With that one lie, many lives were changed. Maisy might have lived in Bluffton forever with Max, and Ruby would have been pampered and loved. But then Ruby would have never met Sal, and Ivy would not have been born. How bizarre to think of that, thought Ivy. She made a note of the place of Max's internment, in a Muskegon cemetery; it would be her next trip, after visiting Maisy's grave, in order to pay her respects for Ruby's sake.

The phone rang, jarring her out of her thoughts. It was Nancy.

"Hey, sorry I couldn't respond sooner. I was busy at work. What's up?"

"Oh, hi Nance. Well, at first I called to see if you wanted to go out with Buddy and me this afternoon, but when I realized you were working, we went alone."

"Where'd you go? Don't tell me you went back to Mary's Boutique and bought that purse we looked at."

"No, actually, I went to the beach in Muskegon."

"Have a good time?"

"Well, yes, -- until I ran into Fox."

"What? What happened? Why was he there? Did he see your son – his son?"

"There's a lot to tell, and you're the best sounding board I have. Is Matt working tonight?"

"Yes, as a matter of fact, he is."

"Good, come over after work, and bring pizza. I'm buying. I already have the Lambrusco. We have a lot to talk about."

"Okay, girlfriend. You've got me curious now. I'll be there as soon as I can get out of here."

"Thanks, Nancy. See ya."

After disconnecting, Ivy realized that Nancy did not know the complete story about Maisy and Max, yet. It was going to be a long night. She decided to take a nap while Buddy was still sleeping. She laid down on the couch with her throw blanket over her legs and Percy curled up next to her, and dreamed of another time when vaudeville was the rage, silent pictures and automobiles were brand new, and Buster Keaton, a local boy, became world famous.

≈

Ivy stretched and yawned. It was going to be difficult to function today. The two women had stayed up late into the night, eating, drinking, talking, and crying together. As usual, Nancy had given very wise advice, but as Ivy recalled their conversation, she wasn't sure she was going to follow it. It would take a lot of courage, and Ivy was not sure she was ready. On the other hand Buddy was growing like a weed, and Fox was missing out.

Nancy had seen right through the issue of Fox's engagement. She said the fact that he was going to get married had nothing to do with anything. He was a father and he had a right to know. If that fact affected his wedding plans, that was up to him and his fiancé. As long as Ivy did not try to come between him and Mandy, but she just informed him that he was Buddy's dad, and she gave him rights to see his son, then neither he nor Buddy could hold anything against her. No doubt he would be upset at first; it was bound to be a shock, but he would get over it, and she was sure he would see she had done the right thing.

Ivy knew she had to do it, but it made her very nervous every time she thought of telling him. And then, there was a matter of how and when. Ivy needed to talk to him alone. This was not a discussion that should include the new woman in his life. The two of them should meet someplace that was neutral ground. Ivy reached over to her nightstand and picked up her phone. She still had his number; she could call. With shaking fingers she hesitated to gather her thoughts and words. Would he pick up after she had ignored his calls so many times? It was probably too early in the day, anyway, she told herself. Maybe later.

Buddy woke up crying, something he rarely did. He seemed to be pretty miserable, so Ivy decided to change his diaper and get him fed as soon as possible. When he wasn't interested in his bottle, she felt his forehead. He was a little warm but not too bad. Then when she inserted her finger in his mouth to check his gums, he clamped down and rubbed his head back and forth. Yes, there it was. A small red bump with a tiny white tooth showing underneath. "Oh my, baby, a tooth! Your first one! Yesterday you learned to sit up by yourself, and your father is not here to see any of this. You're going through new things every day. Yes, Nancy was right. I need to tell him immediately. Forget about his upcoming marriage; I don't know when it is for sure, anyway. They can work that part out for themselves. Now, how will I handle this? Huh, baby?"

As with anything Ivy put her mind to, once she was set on a task, she was like a bloodhound who would not give up the scent. Informing Fox that he was a father was going to happen one way or another.

Chapter Twenty-three

Buddy was fussy all morning. Ivy tried everything she could think of to soothe him; luckily, she had been prepared for this day and had a cold teething ring in the refrigerator. He did enjoy rubbing and biting on it, but he still had outbursts of crying from the pain. Ivy walked the floor with him and then remembered reading about chamomile tea. She made herself a cup to calm her own nerves and then, when it was cooled down, Ivy rubbed some on his gums with her finger. She had to laugh because Buddy couldn't decide if he wanted to gnaw her finger or suck it. Apparently, he really liked chamomile.

When he continued to be fussy and irritated, she decided to try a car ride thinking the hum of the motor and the bouncing of the vehicle would calm him a little;

if that didn't work, she would come back home and walk the floor with him until he passed out from exhaustion.

Today wasn't the bright sunny day that yesterday had been. It was overcast and gray, but it didn't look threatening. Ivy checked her phone weather app, and saw raindrops predicted for this afternoon. If she left now she would be able to get from the apartment building to the car without getting wet.

Packing the diaper bag with everything she could think would be necessary, she prepared Buddy for the drive. So much went into a simple thing like getting in the car for a fifteen-minute trip. "You sure know how to make life complicated, don't you, Bud? Come on, sweets, let's go." As soon as she picked up the car seat, he seemed a little more relaxed. Always curious, his eyes were already scanning the area, looking for something new he had not seen before like a light or a bug or a new color.

"Now, where to? Okay, how about along White Like towards the lighthouse? Sound good?"

It was either the gloomy day or the fact that it was a workday that had kept the traffic down on the road that followed the water's edge, allowing her to drive at a leisurely pace. The gorgeous colors of the trees had turned a tarnished hue overnight, because without the sun to spotlight them, they lacked luster. The bright display of yesterday was not gone for good, though, but only in hiding until the sun came out from behind the heavy cloud layer. The next two weeks would be a hide-and-seek game until the leaves finally grew tired of playing, giving up their clinging hold on the branches they had been a part of for the last six months. Overhead, an odd-shaped V moved across the sky, honking loudly as it went; the flock of geese were moving south toward more weather-friendly grounds where there would be open water the rest of the year.

Ivy tried to take in her surroundings, as it might be the last time she came out this way before winter set in. There were just a few boats on the water; maybe the boaters were getting in their last trip, too. Whatever the view, it didn't matter. Buddy couldn't see out much anyway, but the movement of the car had lulled him enough so at least he was quiet.

When Ivy found herself in front of the driveway leading to her great-grandmother Ruby's cottage, she pulled over and stopped. There wasn't a car around that she could see, and the blinds were closed at the windows. With no one home, she felt safe taking her time, looking over the house. Last fall when she had driven slowly by, there was a pickup truck parked in front, and Fox had come out of the house with a tool in his hands, so she took off. She was not sure if he saw her that day, but that was okay. She had been in no mood to talk to him, anyway. It was shortly before that day that she discovered she was pregnant, and she had not yet decided how she was going to handle telling him, or if she going to tell him at all.

The house looked good; it looked lived in and loved. There was a wheelbarrow propped on the side with a shovel stuck in the ground next to it. A hose was neatly coiled up on a hose reel. Marigolds had been planted around the foundation in small clumps, instead of in a straight row like most people did. Their rusty orange and lemony yellow colors brightened up the landscape, even on this dark day. A sapphire blue ceramic pot of vibrant red geraniums was placed artfully on the steps leading to the screened-in porch, the contrast of colors just perfect with the stain of the wood siding. Someone had used a loving touch when planning the exterior and landscaping. Ivy sighed. How she wished she had been the one to do the planting.

Ivy jumped when someone tapped on her driver's side window. She had not heard the truck pull up behind her or the person approach the car. She was totally embarrassed when she looked into the face of the man she had once loved. He made a motion for her to roll down her window. Ivy glanced nervously back at Buddy, who was completely unaware of the fact that someone very important in his life was so close to him.

Pressing the button, she lowered the glass and looked up sheepishly into that face that could make a girl go weak in the knees. "Hi. I'm sorry, was I blocking your entrance to the house? I was – I – uh – I -- well, I was just looking. Reminiscing, really, about when I was young. You know, when I --"

"Hi to you, too. And don't worry about it. You can look any time you want. Would you like a tour?"

"Ah, no, I have to go. I have --"

"Oh, you're babysitting again! He's a cute little guy. He can come in with you. I don't bite." He smiled a crooked grin.

'Is he flirting?' thought Ivy. 'No, that can't be. He's engaged. The rat!' "No, I think I'd better get him home. He's been fussy; he's teething. Sorry for the intrusion." Fox's face fell with disappointment, but at that exact moment that Ivy put the car into gear, there was a bright flash of lightning with a loud thunderclap right on its heels. Ivy jumped, Buddy screamed, and the skies opened up and dumped on Fox.

"Are you okay?" he asked through the noise of one continuing thunder clap after another. He glanced at Ivy who looked panicked. The baby was in the back seat and couldn't be reached for comforting. "You'd better come in until it blows over. He's terrified."

"Okay, thanks. Can you grab the umbrella in the back seat? Maybe you can hold it over him while we run in."

Fox opened the back door, while Ivy got out and ran to the other side to her son. When she put her head in the back passenger door to extract the boy, he noticed her concerned look; it was a protective and worried expression. Ivy was drenched but working as quickly as she could to get the car seat unfastened. She flipped a blanket over the baby's face, while Fox ran around to her side to shield her from the rain. The deluge of huge heavy drops was cold, driving sideways and beating on their backs. It slammed their bodies with a powerful force, its fierceness pushing them toward the house in a strong horizontal wave. The sound of Buddy's screams could be heard in between the thunder claps.

Fox and Ivy ran together to the door and dove into the screened porch which had been left unlocked. Inside, Fox worked quickly to unlock the interior door.

Once inside he said, "Here, let me take the baby while you take off your coat and shoes."

Ivy hesitated a minute, but then knew she had no choice. Fox caught the look of fear or whatever it was, and wondered what it was about him that so terrified her. As soon as Ivy hung up her jacket, she reached for the baby. Then Fox removed his sport coat and shoes. He had not come dressed to work on the house. Under his jacket he was wearing a white dress shirt and tie, because he had just met with a Realtor in Montague. He glanced at the way Ivy handled the baby. She was so comfortable with the child, and the baby seemed attached to her, too.

"Let me kick on the furnace, and then I'll start a fire in the fireplace."

Buddy began to settle down, now that he was in his mother's arms. She rubbed his back and held him close. "My sweet angel. Were you scared?" she cooed. She walked around a little, bouncing him as she went. "I see you put in a stone fireplace. It looks nice."

"Thanks, but I didn't do it myself. I hired a stone mason. I didn't want to risk burning the house down if I couldn't get the flue to draft right," he chuckled.

"Good thought. Well, it's pretty anyway. I like your choice of layered stone. It's very natural to the outdoor surroundings." Ivy was working hard on small talk. She was so uncomfortable being here, and at the same time she felt as if she never wanted to leave. "What brought you out this way today? Are you staying a while?"

"No, I actually came to see a real estate agent." Fox flushed, and looked down a moment. "I'm thinking of putting her up for sale."

"After all of this work? Was that your plan all along, to flip it?" Her voice was a bit too loud and edgy, and Buddy picked up on her tension, so Ivy tried to relax. She knew she didn't have a right to be angry. He owned the house. He could do what he wanted to with it. Then a thought occurred. "Will you let me know when it goes on the market? I'd like to buy it." She smiled sheepishly at him. "I can afford it now. Royalties, you know."

"Of course I will. Yes, of course – if I decide to sell. I can feel the heat from the furnace now. Would you like to sit? I can make us some coffee. It will only take a few minutes to brew."

"Uh, sure. Yes, that would be fine." The lightning and thunder continued with startling electric flashes followed instantly by symphonic booms, but Buddy was content now that he was inside and could see his mother's face. She rocked him gently back and forth and shortly his eyes grew heavier until he nodded off to the land of baby dreams. Ivy laid him on the couch next to her, since the car seat was drenched, and she propped a pillow next to him to prevent him from rolling off. She gently slid off the smooth leather seat and sat on the floor facing the fireplace, next to him.

Fox sat on the floor opposite of her. "You're good with him," he said.

"Thank you," she responded softly. When she looked up he was staring at her intently. 'Now,' her mind told her, 'now.' Her heart was pounding. It was the perfect time. She would tell him now. "Fox, I have something to tell --"

"Oops, hold that thought. My cell just rang."

He didn't move or take his eyes off of her, as he reached in his pocket for his phone. Ivy could not pull her look away. Tingles ran through her entire body as his eyes casually roamed over her body, seemingly unaware of what he was doing as he talked on the phone. She was wet and disheveled and felt very unattractive. 'Why does he have to be so darned good-looking? And there's that stupid curl, again, just begging to be pushed back.'

"Okay, thank you, I'll stay in touch." He disconnected and put the phone on the floor next to him. "Sorry," he said. "The Realtor again. She really wants this contract." Fox pulled his eyes from hers and glanced at Buddy. "He sure is content now. He's very attached to you. What's his name, by the way? Whose baby is it? Nancy's?"

"We call him Buddy."

"You call him Buddy?"

"Yes, you see, he has a name that turned out to be too big for a baby, really. His actual name is –

"Hold on. That's the ding of the coffeemaker. Cream and sugar? Sorry, I don't have anything to make it chocolate-flavored the way you like it."

"Cream and sugar is fine. Thanks. It's nice that you remembered, though."

He came back with the steaming mugs. "I remember everything, Ivy. Remember the time we got caught in the rain at the lighthouse and went back to your apartment?" He reached out and touched her hand. Ivy jerked back.

"I do," she said a little too strongly. And then added, "Aren't you engaged to be married? Why would you bring that up?"

"Well, actually, I'm not engaged anymore." There was silence as the two locked eyes.

Then Ivy came to her senses and responded, "Since two days ago? What you'd do, scam her out of a house and she caught on?"

"Ivy, that wasn't fair. I never did such a thing to you. But if you must know, I was never really in love with Mandy, and she knew it. She said she always knew, but she didn't care. I was upfront with her from the start. I was looking for companionship, and she was willing to take me as I was. I guess, she thought she could convince me to love her later. I was broken, Ivy. You destroyed me. I loved you more than I ever thought I could love anyone."

Ivy lowered her eyes. She was ashamed at the way she had behaved. Knowing that she had hurt him so much was painful. When she looked back up, she saw tears at the corners of his eyes. He continued on, saying, "When we ran into you at the beach, Mandy saw something in the way I looked at you, and she felt my touch to her hand change while you were there. I was quiet and distracted on the way home. So when we got back to her house, she came out and point-blank asked me if I was still in love with you. She said she didn't mind marrying someone who didn't love her yet, but she would not marry someone who was in love with someone else and would probably never learn to love her. When I confessed that I had never gotten over losing you, she called the whole thing off. She wasn't mad. She blamed herself for pushing me into marriage. We parted friends. She's a very special person, but she's not the girl for me."

There was a quiet pause as Ivy tried to sort through her feelings. "I'm sorry, Fox. I never meant to hurt you. I was just so upset I couldn't see straight. I know now that it wasn't your fault. I think I've grown up a little, ever since I had – well, you know."

"Are you seeing someone, Ivy?"

"No, I'm not. There's been no one since you. I've been too busy, really."

Fox felt his heart flutter with relief. "Would you consider seeing me --"

Buddy started to fuss again, so Ivy moved to attend to him while Fox watched her maternal-like movements, as she propped him on her knees and gently bounced him. 'She'll make a wonderful mother someday,' he thought.

"Say, you never said what the little slugger's real name is."

Ivy sucked in her breath and whispered, "Salvatore."

"Oh sure, after your great-grandfather. But why would Nancy name her son after *your* relative? I read the book, by the way. Really great -- quite mystical, actually. I loved the whole story about the ruby necklace." Ivy misunderstood his blush, thinking because the story was a little sexy, he was embarrassed. But what she didn't know was the blush was because of a secret he held, one he knew he had to tell her. But not yet. He needed to move the subject away from the book for the moment, so he turned the conversation back to the baby. "So, did Nancy love the name so much that she wanted to use it?"

"What? No." Ivy took a deep breath and forged ahead. "Fox, his name is Salvatore Morton."

"Morton? What? He's your kid? Why didn't you say so? You said you were babysitting. I don't understand."

"I was embarrassed, I guess, not being married and all. You see, he's six months old, Fox. He was born in April of this year."

Fox frowned, wondering what she was saying, and then he dropped his jaw. He was trying to do some backwards math, but was lost in the numbers and the confusion. "Ivy, what are you telling me?"

"I'm telling you that the name on his birth certificate is actually Salvatore Fox Marzetti." Ivy didn't realize she had begun to cry. Tears rolled silently down her cheeks as she held her son close. This was the moment that would change everything. And how Fox handled the news depended on whether she would allow Buddy's father to see him on a weekly basis, and if that happened, it meant she would have to forfeit precious moments of her son's life to someone else.

"He's mine? I – don't know what to say. I – uh – I – you went through it all alone without telling me? How could you? I would have been there for you! I would have gone to doctor's appointments and ultrasounds. Did you mistrust me that much that you were willing to withhold my own flesh and blood from me?" Then he reached out and demanded, "Let me hold my son." When Fox realized his voice had come out more sternly than he had planned, he softened his tone. "Can I hold him, please?"

Ivy kissed her baby boy and handed him to his father. Fox held him high in the air while studying his round little face. He saw himself, his father, and generations before him. Buddy broke out in a big toothless grin, then erupted with a giggle coming from deep down in his belly and soul, in a primal recognition of his father. Fox pulled him to his chest as he sobbed, "My son."

Chapter Twenty-four

For over a half hour, father and son played together. Fox poked and tickled, and made silly faces and noises. Buddy loved every second, and when the baby needed a change, Fox said, "Let me."

"Really?" asked Ivy in surprise.

"I have a lot of family. There's always a baby around. I've always known how to change a diaper," he stated. Ivy noticed a coolness when he talked to her, which wasn't there before she had told him about Buddy.

Fox ignored Ivy and took complete charge of the baby. She sat quietly by and watched. He was focused one hundred percent on his child as he tried to soak up every precious second. He began taking pictures with his phone; he couldn't stop clicking shots. For him it was like the first day his son was born. Then, when Buddy's eyes began to get droopy, he laid down with him on the couch, rubbing his son's back until the baby fell asleep, Buddy's aching gums soothed by something much greater than medicine.

When the child had finally drifted off, Fox eased himself up, and stood next to the couch for a few moments watching his newly discovered offspring sleep. Then he turned with cold eyes on Ivy, and said, "We need to talk."

The two parents sat at the table with freshly filled cups of coffee. The thunder and lightning had settled down, the worst of the storm now distant rumbles away, but the rain was still heavy, driven in windy bursts. It didn't matter the weather, but now that the truth had come out, staying in the house gave them a perfect reason to work things out and come to some sort of agreement.

Ivy was silent, not knowing how to begin. She had gone through a range of emotions while watching Fox play with Buddy. Fox studied the woman he thought he loved; he *did* love. She hadn't changed a bit since he had seen her last October. She had the same sun-streaked-hair that made a man yearn to run his fingers through it. She was a bit thinner, probably from trying to work and raise a baby at the same time alone, but her figure was still curvy in all the right places. At the moment her eyes were dulled and tear-filled. She seemed embarrassed and ashamed, and very nervous. One part of him yearned to wrap his arms around her and make sweet love to her in front of the fireplace the way they had done when they most probably had conceived Buddy, while another part of him was furious at her for her deception.

"Fox, I –

"Ivy, I —

They both began at the same time. Then Fox nodded her way. "You go first, and it had better be good."

"I'm not sure what to say, except that I *am* sorry. As I said before, I was hurt and embarrassed. And to be honest, I was being stubborn. I can see that now.

Nancy begged me to tell you; in fact, she's the reason your name is on the birth certificate. She convinced me that Buddy would want to know when he was older, if I had not told you by then."

"Well, thank you for that much, at least."

"You see, I truly had no plans of ever telling you in the beginning, but once I had finished writing Ruby and Sal, I began to feel the connection to family more and more. Ruby had no one but a lousy father growing up. That much we know is true because she told me so herself. But it wasn't until recently when I came into some new facts and started to research the story for my next book, that I discovered what withholding a child's father can mean, and how it affects the lives of others. I began to worry what Buddy would think of me when he discovered I knew where to find his father all along. I realized that he had an extended family of aunts, uncles, cousins, and grandparents that could be beneficial in his life."

Fox had been slouching over his cup, not looking at her as she talked, but at the mention of grandparents, he jerked up. "Grandparents! My mom and dad! I can't wait to tell them." His face went through a range of emotions -- from to joy, to pain, to anger. Ivy longed to reach over and comfort him. He was such a beautiful man, and now she could see what a loving and compassionate person he was.

"I'm going to need to see him regularly, Ivy. I know it will be hard, because I live on the other side of the state, but I have to have bonding time with him."

"Yes, I see that now. You're right, of course."

"I'll want to take him to see my family. Will you be okay with me taking him to Bay City?"

"Today? Absolutely not!"

"No, I didn't mean today, but sometime soon."

"Possibly. I'm not sure how this works," said Ivy. "Do we need to go to court?"

"Only if we can't work it out by ourselves. I'll support him financially, also. We'll need to talk money, soon, but I want you to come to me for anything you need for him. Is that understood?"

"Yes, but Fox, I'm doing quite well with the book sales, and uh – I came into an inheritance, so I'm good."

Fox said firmly, "I don't care how much money you make. I'm going to take care of my son! You can keep your stupid book money to yourself. I don't want him to ever think I didn't want to be in his life. I truly can't believe you did this to me! I'll see him whenever I'm on this side of the state. I *will* see him every other weekend for sure, and by that I mean I will *take* him with me. I will have the standard alternating holidays, so he can learn about my family's traditions. He'll grow up as a Marzetti, not a Morton. And from now on, I will call him by his traditional Italian name; Sal. Buddy can be used as a nickname at home, but when he goes to school, he will be called Sal."

Up until this point, the discussion had been emotional but civil at times, but now Fox had pushed a button with Ivy. He was beginning to sound like her father, making demands, and that would not do. She would not let anyone talk to her like that. He had no right to bark out orders.

"Well, that's it. I'm done. Rain or not, I'm leaving. I had already decided to give you shared custody, but you will not tell me what to do with my child."

In true Italian fashion, Fox raised his voice. "Your child? Yours? He's mine, too, which you neglected to tell me about until today. And what if we had not been caught in a rain storm, would you have *ever* told me?" Fox pounded the table, but when he saw Ivy flinch, he became ashamed of himself. He couldn't remember when he had last lost his temper like that. The Italian way of speaking in loud voices wasn't for everyone. He saw that it was time to take it down a notch.

"Okay, I'm sorry for getting loud; it's a family trait. But we need to figure this out. How about this? I'll take time off; I'll take the rest of this week. I'll tell my boss and family that I need to do some repairs, here. I won't go back until next Monday morning, that's eight days away. Until then, do I have your permission to spend time with Buddy – Sal?"

Ivy bit her lip the way she always did when she was working out a problem. Even in his anger, Fox was so attracted to her it hurt. He remembered what those lips could do to a man; she could be sexy as all get out. But she could also look like a little girl at times, lost and needy. She had such an innocence about her, but now he saw a new side to her; a lioness, capable of being fiercely protective of her son.

"Okay," she said thoughtfully. "Are you staying here, tonight?"

"Yes, I'm not selling the house now. It's a perfect place to live when I visit him. I'm calling the agent as soon as you leave. It's not going on the market."

Ivy sighed with relief. She would not have a chance to buy the cottage, but maybe Buddy could still inherit it. In that way, it would stay in the family, keeping its stories with the bloodline. But it would have to be without her, because with one look at Fox's face, she could tell that he hated her now. She had destroyed what love was lingering from last year. For a moment she had allowed herself to wonder if maybe there was a chance, but that was gone. She always managed to make a mess of things, and she had done it big time, here.

"All right, I'm taking Buddy home now. He's had it rough, lately, with the teething and all. I'll call you in the morning, and we can work something out for the week. Is that acceptable?"

"Yes, that's fine. And Ivy, I'm not keeping this a secret. As soon as we work out arrangements, I'm introducing him to my family."

"I understand. And you should. I want Buddy to have a wonderful experience with family around him as he's growing up. It's something I never had. So yes, you should tell them." She carried her untouched coffee to the sink, and then went to her sleeping infant, while Fox watched her every move. Buddy never woke as she bundled him for the drive home. Once she had her own coat and shoes on, she picked up the baby carrier, and walked to the door. Fox bent over to kiss his son goodbye. His head was next to her chest. She ached to touch him. She ached to pull him to her breast. She ached to kiss him. She ached.

"Thank you for telling me, Ivy. I appreciate it." He leaned over the carrier and kissed her gently on the cheek. She simply nodded and walked out the door.

Chapter Twenty-five

"Nancy, can you come over, please? I need you."
Ivy was crying into the phone, and in a matter of
seconds her loyal friend was right there. Buddy was
sitting in his high chair pushing toys off the tray as fast
as Ivy put them back on. His new game never ceased to
make him laugh.

"Well, at least Buddy is happy. What's up,
honey?"

"I saw Fox today at the cottage. I told him. I told
him everything."

"You did? Why, that's wonderful! I'm so proud of
you. What happened? How did he take it?"

"He was angry with me, as I suspected he would
be, but the instant he held Buddy, he softened. They

bonded immediately. It was really quite something to see. Buddy's crazy about him."

"Perfect. That's what we hoped for. So what's the problem?"

"He's calling me today to set up a custody arrangement. I'll have to give up Buddy every other weekend, most likely, and he wants to take him to Bay City to meet his family. I don't think I can bear to let him out of my control for that long." Ivy began to sob, already missing her son before he even left.

"You'll have to, Ivy. If you don't go along with it, he'll probably take you to court, and things could get messy. Besides, Buddy will love all of the extra attention, and you'll have free time to write. It's a win/win."

"I know you're right. I just have to get used to the idea."

"Good girl. So, what's next?"

"He'll call me this afternoon, and see if we can work things out."

"Okay, good. But what about Fox, himself? How did you feel being near him again?"

Ivy finally chuckled. "He's as good-looking as ever. What female with a pulse wouldn't want to be near him? But as far as the two of us, I think he's done with me – although he is no longer engaged and at one point he did say he still loved me, but then everything blew up." Ivy went over every detail word for word so Nancy could get the full picture. Then after a few hours, when the phone rang with Fox's call, Nancy signaled that she was leaving so Ivy could have privacy.

The sound of his voice made her heart pound. She finally admitted to herself that she was still in love with him. "Sorry to bother you so soon, but I've made a long list of items I will need in order to keep Buddy here. Do you have a few minutes to go over it with me? I'm going shopping in the morning, and then I'm going to set up his own room."

"That's nice. Sure, I have some time. What do you need to know?"

"Well, I know the main things like a crib and a highchair, but smaller items and diaper size and brand, I don't have a clue about. I'll need your help."

"Okay, got a pen? Tell me what you have so far."

The next few minutes was spent discussing baby items, and then the talk worked its way to more personal things about their lives, and what they had been doing since they had last seen each other. They steered clear of Fox's relationship with Mandy, but they chatted about everything else from his job to Ivy's book. Ivy even told him a small bit about meeting Ronnie and the new book project. It was so comfortable, talking with him again. At the end of the conversation, Ivy had agreed to take Buddy to him late in the afternoon the next day, giving him time to buy everything necessary to take care of an infant. She laughed when she hung up, because she had never heard of a man who was so excited about baby shopping.

≈

Fox was more nervous than a turkey at Thanksgiving dinner. He was more nervous than a long-tailed cat in a room full of rocking chairs. He was more nervous than a pig in a bacon factory. He was just plain nervous. The baby room was set up, with a new crib and changing table. He had also purchased a car seat, a Pack 'n Play, and a high chair, two mobiles, a few toys and rattles, and a stuffed bear. Luckily, the woman in the baby store had been most helpful, because he had completely forgotten about the sheets for the crib and a tub and towels for bathing. After loading up his pickup, he had hauled everything in and then began the task of putting the crib and changing table together, which was not as easy as he thought it would be, even for a handyman like himself. But now he was finally ready, and he was pacing the floor with anticipation.

"Where is she?" he said aloud. "I thought she was coming at three." He paced a few more times and when he heard the car, he almost came out of his skin. Fox ran outside to help Ivy carry Buddy in, along with the diaper bag and some of Buddy's clothing she said she was bringing along. When he got to the car, his grin was so wide it looked like his face was going to crack.

Greeting Ivy was somewhat awkward, but since she was already busy getting the baby carrier out of the car, he had been able to avoid the problem of whether he should hug or kiss her. The trio went inside, looking to all the rest of the world as a happy family. Ivy couldn't help but be impressed with Fox's eagerness to be with Buddy.

"Here you go, baby. We're inside now. Go see your daddy," she said as she handed the carrier to him.

Fox's head jerked. "Daddy," he said quietly. "That's the first time I've heard that word relating to me. Thank you for saying that, Ivy. I appreciate it."

Whenever he made a comment like that or showed his excitement over being a father, Ivy's heart melted a little more towards him; but mostly she felt shame at keeping her secret for so long. She was bound and determined to make up for any wrong she had done.

"Hi, Buddy, let me get you out of that thing. I want to carry you around and show you your room. How's that?"

The little guy laughed with delight at being picked up by Fox. He reached out to grab his nose and search his face with his hands, even poking at his eyes, then he settled in for the warmth of his father's chest. "How is the teething going? He seems okay, now."

"Oh, exciting news. There's a tooth. Look!" Ivy pulled Buddy's lip down. "Right here on the bottom."

"I see it. Congratulations, baby boy. Real food is coming soon. You're on your way to becoming a man."

"Oh please, no, don't remind me," moaned Ivy as the parents laughed together about their son.

"Okay, so this is how I set everything up. What do you think?" Fox was ready for constructive criticism. He was like a duck out of water when it came to decorating and making decisions about baby furniture placement.

"Everything looks really nice, but you might want to move the crib away from the window. Too much draft in the summer, and the glass gets too cold in the winter."

"Okay, good. I hadn't thought of that." And on it went, as they discussed onesies, socks, diapers, lotion, bathing soap, etc.

"I bought this bouncy chair that converts to a swing. Do you think he'd like to try it? It even plays music."

"Let's try. He really likes movement." And Buddy did like it. At first he kicked his legs to make it go, and then after a time his eyes got heavy and he began to drift off.

"Do you want to stay a bit? I'm really not sure I'm ready to be left alone with him quite yet. I might need you to show me the ropes when it comes to feeding."

"Oh, okay, I guess I can. I had already started weaning him to a bottle, because I might have to travel for the book soon, so that works out perfectly for you. I brought some of his formula along, and we can go over his feeding schedule. But basically, I feed him when he's hungry and let him sleep when he's tired. He's a pretty happy baby. He only cries when he's hungry, wet, or sick."

"Well, it's all new to me. Can I get you anything? Coffee, tea, pop?"

"Just water, please."

Fox and Ivy moved to the couch, sitting side by side, as they watched their son sleep. They talked the afternoon away, Ivy answering every question Fox could think of about Buddy. He even asked about his birth and if there was a video. The low voices they were speaking in created a feeling of closeness. Fox saw the girl he had first met when her scarf had entangled his feet, her hair blowing in the wind as small strands whipped across her face, pointing out her luscious lips. His heart swelled, and he felt a desire to hold her close to him once again. He longed to kiss her, but he knew she was still resentful because he had purchased her great-grandmother's house before she had a chance to do so herself. He had never been able to tell her why, or that he was still holding back a secret. He would need to ease into it, the same way she had when she had told him about his son.

Ivy's heart was beating so hard she was sure that Fox could hear it. His closeness was causing her to suck in ragged breaths and as the air escaped her body, it felt like there was not enough coming back in to compensate. She felt light-headed, but would not let him know it. She knew he was not interested in starting up with her again. Maybe Mandy was not the one for him, but he had made it clear that she was not either, hadn't he?

"Ivy –

"Yes?"

"I – uh – I'm not going to be ready to take Buddy alone right away. Can you come with him again tomorrow? Let me take over the baby duties and you just watch and supervise to make sure I'm doing everything right." Fox knew that once he had Buddy's schedule down, he could handle it alone; he had done plenty of babysitting for younger cousins when he was a teen, but he was not about to tell Ivy that.

"Sure, I can stay tomorrow, if you like." More time with Fox is all she had been thinking about today. "When should I come back?"

"Let's make a day of it – you know -- so I can see how his daily routine goes."

"Oh, okay. I'm free all day tomorrow. Is nine o'clock too early? I can bring him unbathed so you can help with that, too."

"Perfect," he responded.

'Yes, perfect,' she thought.

Chapter Twenty-six

As soon as Ivy and Buddy were gone, Fox felt deflated; where a moment ago he was happy and fulfilled, he was now empty. He needed more than his son to make him happy; he needed them both – mother *and* child. He would never feel complete unless he could work this out, and Buddy might be the catalyst to bringing them back together.

Fox's mother had known about Ivy ever since the weekend Ivy and Fox had gone to the White Lake lighthouse and gotten soaked in a rainstorm. She knew he was different when he came back to Bay City, happier than he had ever been before, and she had grilled him until he caved. Each time he had someone he thought was special, the rest of the family wouldn't leave him alone about it, asking questions he didn't want to answer. This time he kept it a secret from everyone but his mother and his brother-in-law, Jarrod, who had helped him work on the house and had been sworn to secrecy, because by that time Fox was miserable over losing her. Fox glanced at his laptop, knowing it was time to break the news. He flipped it open and clicked on the Skype icon. His mother answered right away, always eager to keep track of her children.

"Hey, Mom, how're you doing?"

"Well, I'm fine, but what about you? Are you okay? You usually just call or text unless you're out of town for a long time. But, don't get me wrong, I can never get enough of that face."

Fox laughed. His family was everything to him. "I'm good. In fact, I'm wonderful. I wanted to see your faces, because I have some news. Is Dad around?"

"Yes, but he's in the garage. Let me get him." Fox heard shuffling and then his mother calling, "Hank? Are you out there? Come on in. It's Fox. He wants to talk to us."

Fox heard, "My hands are all greasy; can't you just tell me about it?"

"Come on. Wash your hands. It won't take long."

After some splashing sounds, Fox's father came into the picture. "How are you, son?"

"Good, Dad. Adjust the computer so you can sit down."

"Are you in trouble?" asked Hank.

"No, nothing like that. Okay. All set? Mom, I can't see your face. Get in the picture."

"Oh, is that better?"

"Perfect," said Fox. "Now, I told you I've decided to stay here for a week and get some things done around my cottage."

"Yes, -- you didn't get hurt did you?" asked his mother.

"No, no. I'm fine. Now let me tell you the rest without interruption, okay?

"Okay, Fox, go ahead." Fox could see his mother was still worried, so he forged ahead to get right to the point. First, he had to explain to his father about Ivy, but it turned out his mother had already filled him in about that part. Then he went on to tell about how the cottage had been willed to her first before he had purchased it, and how he had fallen head over heels in love with her, and then she had broken his heart. Next, he had to explain why he had broken his engagement to Mandy. He had expected that to be the difficult part, but he was quite surprised with the response he got.

"Well, that's a good thing," his mother clicked her tongue. "That girl was never right for you, anyway; we all knew it."

"You did? As it turns out, you were right about that. After Mandy and I ran into Ivy, I saw Ivy again, another accidental meeting. She was with her son. They got caught in a rainstorm near my house, so I invited them in. After some time, Ivy owned up to something very special. Are you ready?"

"Hurry up, the suspense is killing us," said his mother.

Hank said, "Get on with it, son; I need to get back to my project."

"Mom and Dad, I'm a father. Ivy's son is mine. He's almost seven months old and he's wonderful. He's perfect, in fact."

"But – how—well, we know how, but are you sure?" they both said at the same time.

"There's no doubt. He looks like me and the whole Marzetti clan, but to satisfy you all, we'll do a DNA test. I've got lots of pictures. I'll send them right away."

"Oh, Fox," said his mother as she choked back tears, "I never thought I would see this day."

"A new grandbaby?" said his dad. "Nothing could be better! When can we meet him?"

"I've only been with him twice, but I'm spending the day with him tomorrow. Ivy's teaching me the ropes. She's giving me shared custody, so I can either bring him home to you, or you can come to me here."

"Try to keep me away!" said his mother. "Call us every night and tell us all about him. And pictures – lots of pictures. Oh, and can I tell everyone else?'

"Tell the whole world, Mom. You're a grandma again!"

When the goodbyes were done and the pictures had been sent, Fox sat alone in his kitchen. He couldn't stop grinning. Then he rose to go into the bedroom to change his clothes. He wanted to turn off the outside spigots for the winter before it got dark. As Fox stepped on the board that Sal had pried up over one hundred years ago, it squeaked. The sound was a reminder of what was hidden beneath. Standing there, on top of that secret place, Fox felt the warmth run up his leg. He had not felt that sensation for quite a while. Was it time? He bent down and lifted the board to reveal a small box. When he opened the box, the ruby and diamond necklace was so brilliant, he was almost blinded. When he first discovered the necklace under the safe last fall, he had felt this same warm electric vibration, but after a time, the sensation stopped. Whenever Fox would work on the cottage, he would check on the necklace to make sure it was still there. It soon became a reminder of Ivy that hurt too much to look at, so he stopped handling it. Then, one day, after he was engaged to Mandy, when he lifted the loose board and looked at the rubies once more, they were dull. He picked it up, expecting the same electric vibration as had always been there, but the stones were cold and lifeless.

"Now, I get it," he said out loud, a mystery finally solved. "It only works for Ivy. She's the one. You chose her for me, didn't you? Are you saying that my love story will be like Ruby and Sal's? If that's the case, I'm all in."

Fox sat on the bed, with the rubies entwined through his fingers. This necklace had been left in the house after Sal had died, and Ruby, Ivy's great-grandmother, had moved into town. Sal had hidden it under the safe, but Ruby was never able to find it. Ivy searched, too, because she had been told the story by her great-grandmother, and then she had turned that story into a best-selling novel. After Fox had purchased the house and he had made the discovery, the first thing he wanted to do was to give it to Ivy, because he had figured out that the day Ivy left him for good, she had been looking for the rubies in the cellar. Upon reading

Ivy's book, most people assumed the story about the necklace was fiction, but Sal had been lucky enough to know the truth, and now Fox did, too. It was a sign. Magic, fantasy, enchantment, whatever you wanted to call it, Fox knew the truth. The necklace was working its seductive pull, drawing Fox and Ivy together, and he was going to do everything he could to help make that happen.

Chapter Twenty-seven

For once everything went like clockwork. Buddy was more than happy to cooperate for his big day. He had been changed and fed, and was now loaded in the car. Ivy was a little nervous about what she had agreed to. A whole day with Fox could be awkward – or it could be wonderful. It was completely up to him. Ivy was ready to take it in whatever direction he chose. She would let him take the lead.

Fox had been looking out the window, watching for their arrival, so when the car pulled up, he came right out to help with Buddy and the large amount of paraphernalia that went with him.

"Hi, you're right on time!"

"Yes, for a change. Here, can you help with this? Thanks. Oh, and I brought a stroller along. I noticed you didn't have one. I have a large one that works with the car seat, and I was given this lightweight umbrella type as a shower gift. You can have it."

"Why, thank you, Ivy. That's very thoughtful. Come on, let's get this big guy inside. Hi, Bud. Gonna spend the day with Daddy?"

The day went flying by. Fox and Ivy did not have one cross word the entire time. She walked him through the bath, and made lists of Buddy's likes and dislikes. She had photocopied his shot record, and had given him the name and number of his pediatrician. She had even brought him a video that Nancy had made during Buddy's birth, an ultrasound photo from when she was first pregnant, and other shots of her and the baby as soon as he was born. Fox never once criticized her for not telling him about her pregnancy earlier.

As soon as Buddy was settled for his midmorning nap, they collapsed – Ivy on the couch and Fox on the overstuffed chair.

"Wow, he sure can keep you busy," said the exhausted new father.

Ivy was amazed. He had been so eager to learn everything, and he put so much effort into it, that she had no doubt he could be trusted with her son – their son. "The thing is, once you get used to having him around, you can let him play in his chair or playpen, and you can do other things. As long as you stay where you can keep an eye on him at all times. I quite often write with him playing next to me. He's happiest if he can see you. He just likes to know that you're there."

"That's good to know. I don't think I can keep up that pace all day long."

"Fox," asked Ivy, "how will you handle him when you're working? Do you only want him on weekends or weekday evenings?"

"I tossed and turned all night about how I would deal with seeing him while I'm living on the other side of the state. I told my parents, by the way, and they are ecstatic, over the moon, in fact. They can't wait to meet him -- and you, of course."

"Not sure I'm ready for that, yet. They probably aren't fond of how I handled things. We'll see. So what did you decide about taking him to Bay City?"

"I've made a pretty big decision. I made a call this morning and talked to my boss. I told him I was turning in my resignation. I have a scheduled appraisal next week, and after that I'm moving here to the cottage permanently. He was shocked, but when I explained that I loved this side of the state and had been thinking of moving here for quite some time, he said he understood. I didn't mention Buddy. I didn't think that part was his business."

Ivy watched Fox talk. He was animated and excited with his decision. It was the perfect solution as far as she was concerned; she would not have to watch as Buddy was taken many miles away every other weekend. But what about Fox, she wondered. "That's a big sacrifice. Are you sure? What will you do for work?"

"That's the other exciting part. I'm hanging out my shingle and going into business for myself. I've thought about it off and on over the years, and now I'm going to go ahead and do it. It's perfect for all of us. I've got banking contacts here already. I'll try to get in with some of them for mortgage appraisals to start. Later, I hope to pick up private clients. I can work from home for some of it, and if I have Buddy, I just won't accept an appraisal job during that time."

"That's wonderful. I would be more than willing to work with you on the scheduling. We wouldn't have to be stuck to weekends only that way. You might be able to help me out, too, when I have to travel for a book signing. I never wanted to do that, but now I'm told I'll have to."

"Yeah, I can see it will be perfect for everyone, and Buddy is the biggest beneficiary. He'll have both of his parents nearby at all times." Fox thought that something else should be said, but he wasn't quite sure how to work it in. He lowered his voice to a more intimate level, and said, "You know, you're always welcome here. This house was meant for you, anyway."

"Yes, well, sadly that didn't work out for me."

"You mentioned that you would be ready to buy it from me, but now if I stay, I won't be selling. Does that upset you?"

Ivy took a deep breath. She saw Fox's concern for her. Could Nancy have been right all along? Maybe Fox had never had any intention of hurting her. She looked across the room and saw a kind and loving man, someone who was gentle with his son. "No, it doesn't upset me, anymore. I've come to terms with it. You bought it fair and square."

"You know," said Fox quietly, he was standing near the fireplace now, arm resting on the mantle, foot on the hearth, "I bought this house for you."

Ivy looked up, questioning what he had just said. The curl had escaped to his forehead again. He looked all the world like Clark Gable without a moustache in that famous 'Gone with the Wind' poster or perhaps Pierce Brosnan as James Bond. His sexuality was unnerving. There was silence as Ivy tried to comprehend what he was saying.

"You did what?"

Fox slowly moved towards her without responding at first, then he slid down to the spot next to her. Taking her hands in his, he said again, "I bought it for you."

"But – why – I don't understand."

"Ivy, I was crazy in love with you. I knew you couldn't afford to buy it, or so I thought. I knew you were devastated at losing your heritage. So I bought it with the intention of giving it to you no matter what, but I was hopeful you would marry me, and we would live in it together, as Ruby and Sal had."

"You didn't just want it because it was an Al Capone house?"

"Well, that sure made things interesting, but it wasn't that important. I wanted to make you happy. When I saw the bids going up and up and then you dropped out, I was determined to get it no matter the cost. I'm not wealthy, but I had money put aside, and I knew I could cover it."

Ivy began to cry, covering her face with her hands. She had so misjudged this man. She had made a mess of the past year and a half. If she had only given him a chance to explain, they could have been together this whole time. And things would have been so different.

Fox eased his arm around her, afraid she might reject him. He wasn't sure if she was upset or ashamed, but either way he enjoyed the closeness, her warmth was intoxicating. He inhaled her hair; it held the lemony fragrance of his dreams. She lowered her face to his chest. He loved holding her this way, but he gently pushed her away and wiped her tears with his thumbs, then he lowered his face to hers and kissed her sweet lips. They were nectar; they were honey; they were sugar cane.

Ivy could feel Fox's heart beating next to hers. Their rhythm was completely in sync. She had missed him so much. Ivy moaned softly and submitted to his caresses. His hands stroked her chin and then moved to her neck. He began to unbutton her blouse so he could free what was hidden beneath. She was willing. She needed him as much as he needed her. She tipped her head back and allowed access to what he was seeking, but an infant's wail in the next room interrupted them. Naptime was over.

They stopped for a moment, both breathing heavily. Fox continued kissing her, not wanting to give up on what he had started. Ivy laughed softly, as she pushed him away. "Boys will be boys. Both of you."

"Give me a moment," said Fox, huskily. "I'll take care of him."

Ivy left the two of them alone, and while Fox was handling Buddy, most likely changing a diaper, she roamed through the house, taking a good look at the changes that had been made. She loved the whole concept. She took a peek inside his room, the one Ruby and Sal had slept in a century ago. She could still hear Fox's voice talking to Buddy, so she stepped inside. It looked like the same bedframe and headboard that Ruby had left behind – she was sure of it. As she neared the bed to run her fingers over the wrought iron, she stepped on that loose board she had pulled up when she was searching for the hidden money. She stopped, frozen. At that moment a warm tingling sensation filled her body; she felt slightly dizzy. She must have been channeling her great-grandmother, because she could see her face right in front of her. Ruby was gesturing, almost pleading. Was Ruby trying to tell her something? Ivy was standing next to the bed where the Prohibition-era couple had made love with a dazzle of sparkling rubies between them. She thought she heard the word 'Fox' in an echo-like whisper. The sound bounced around the room. Was Fox the man Ivy was meant to be with? She knew now that he was still attracted to her. She definitely knew that she was attracted to him. She didn't want to assume that because they had a child together that they would automatically be a couple for life, but wasn't that what she wanted? Hadn't she been dreaming about that very thing, if she was honest with herself?

"What do you think?"

Ivy jumped, embarrassed at being caught standing in his bedroom. Fox didn't seem to notice or care that he had surprised her. She smiled as she saw him holding Buddy. Poor baby, his shirt was on backwards, and one sock had fallen off, but the snaps at the shoulder were secure. The diaper looked like it was on properly, at least. Buddy grinned when he saw his mother. She reached for him, but he turned his head and buried his face in his father's neck. A strong bond had already begun to form.

"I'm sorry. I shouldn't have come into your room, but I saw Ruby's headboard. I wanted to touch it, I guess."

"No problem. I tried to keep the integrity of the place; I felt the historical significance was important, so I kept whatever antiques were left behind. There were a lot of things I had to change to modernize and bring up to code, but I couldn't part with the headboard. After reading 'Ruby and Sal,' I was glad I hadn't."

He looked at her longingly and then the bed, but he was holding his son, and nothing could be done about his desires now. She smiled, her knees almost giving out with the sensual call to her heart. Fox saw her sway, and glancing down, he noticed that her feet were planted on the loose board. He grinned. He was right; the magic had begun. He stepped forward, and taking her by the elbow, he gently moved her to the next room, before they did something in front of Buddy that was completely inappropriate.

Chapter Twenty-eight

The evening sky was darkening; the air was damp, but sweet with autumnal decay from the rotting leaves and withering plants. A few crickets and tree frogs merged their high-pitched notes as their songs echoed over the lake, but other than that there was silence, as most of the birds had already left for the winter. A raucous crow screamed in the woods, calling out his scavenged find to his flock, and a single mourning dove softly fluttered its wings as it settled in the nearby white pine for the night; both would spend their winter here.

The sleeping baby had already been secured into the back seat, his head lolling sideways, his drooling mouth hanging open. Fox and Ivy were standing next to her car door, saying their goodbyes.

"I had a wonderful time, Fox."

"I did, too. Thank you for today. You've been more than generous with Buddy."

"Well, I have a lot of making up to do. I think we can work this custody thing out, so it should go smoothly. Buddy will never know he's any different than one of his friends living in a two-parent home."

There was a pause as Fox decided how to deal with the next step. 'No, not yet,' he thought. 'This is not the time.'

"I'm going to go to Muskegon to the courthouse tomorrow to apply for a business license, and then I'll stop at a printing store to order business cards and invoices with my name on it. As soon as that order comes in, I can begin to pursue clients."

"Will there be a problem with you taking some of your old firm's business?"

"No, I'll stay away from Medicaid claims. There's enough business out there for new home purchasers, and my company never did that type of work over here, anyway. I'll be okay. I might be broke for a while, but I should be doing fine by spring. That's when houses are beginning to move again; there's always such a long wait for appraisals that they should be happy to see me coming. I can't wait to be on my own, actually." Fox took a step closer to Ivy. The moon was shining on her face, highlighting the streaks of her hair and the oval shape of her eyes. He needed to be close. He needed to feel her body touching his. He reached out for her hand and caressed her knuckles. The sensation sent shivers through her body.

"Uh, well, that's good. Um, what will you name your business? Have you thought about it yet?"

"I knew it the moment I conceived the idea in the middle of the night. I'm going to call it Marzetti and Son."

"That's perfect, Fox." Ivy's eyes filled once again, as they had been doing so often, lately. She berated herself for withholding the baby from him for so long. He was a very special man.

"I know what you're thinking; it's really okay, Ivy. Many men have been in the military when their child is born, and they bond as soon as they come home. I haven't missed out on the big things -- yet -- like first steps, first words, and first ballgame." Fox stepped closer, pressing his body to hers, wrapping his arm around her waist. He could feel the rounded curves she had to offer. He already knew how their softness would conform to his flat male chest; he had spent one glorious weekend exploring every inch of her. He ached to do the same right now. "What's the plan for tomorrow?" he asked as he nibbled on her ear.

"I haven't thought about it, have you?" Ivy was having trouble thinking. Her heart was racing so fast she was sure he could hear it.

"I thought,"—he kissed her brow, -- "you could bring Buddy" -- he kissed her eyes --"for supper" -- he kissed her nose -- "and he could stay the night." He kissed her lips. She wrapped her arms around him, standing on her toes to make contact with all the right places. The kiss was sweet and tender, two lovers discovering each other after a long separation. "And maybe you might like to stay, too. What do you think?" They were breathing heavily. The kissing had turned to a passion they had begun in the house earlier and had not been able to complete.

When Ivy could catch her breath, she pushed away slightly. "Fox, this is wonderful, but are we moving too quickly? Shouldn't we take it one step at a time? Let's see how the day goes. Okay?"

Fox pulled her back in, and cradled her head on his chest. He whispered, "You're right. We have a lot to talk about, still. If you want to stay in the guest room, I'll understand."

Ivy looked into his gorgeous face, the planes of his cheek bones and jawline demanded her caress. "We'll see. No promises. I don't want this to be only about Buddy. We can't be together just because of him. It has to be right for us, too."

"It *is* right for us. You'll see. I'm going to explain it all tomorrow." Ivy studied him questioningly. What could he possibly have to say to her? They shared one last lingering kiss goodbye; parting was almost impossible.

Ivy laughed. "We're acting like teenagers making out at the end of a date. I really have to get home before Buddy wakes up, or I'll have to put him to sleep all over again. We'll come back tomorrow at five. How's that?"

"I'll be counting the minutes," he said with a low husky voice, as he looked longingly at her. She opened the car door, sat down, and started the engine, but before putting the car in gear, she rolled down the window for one last taste of his lips.

The following day dragged on for Ivy. She tended to Buddy, cleaned house, did some laundry, and then called Nancy to tell her that she wouldn't be home that night, and asked her to feed Percy in the morning. Every time Ivy thought about what Fox had suggested, she got nervous, wondering if she was doing the right thing. She resolved to stick with her decision to stay in the guest room, positive she would be doing what was right for Buddy and not what she wanted with every fiber of her being. Of course, Buddy would have no knowledge of what went on once he was asleep, one way or the other, but the results of spending a night with Fox too early could be disastrous for everyone. Ivy had never been one to jump into bed with a man easily, and even though this time was different because she had a history with Fox, she decided that taking things slowly was for the best.

Fox woke up full of excitement and anticipation. No matter what Ivy chose to do as far as sleeping arrangements, he would have his family under one roof all night long – and he did already think of them as his family. He knew it was dangerous to think that way, in case Ivy changed her mind about him, especially after he told her his secret, but for the rest of his life he would always consider them both to be his. They were meant for each other, plain and simple.

After having a light breakfast of cereal and toast, he showered and dressed in a business-like fashion, with a sport jacket and dress slacks; then before going out the door he covered his head with his favorite fedora. There only a few men who could pull off this look; he was one of the lucky ones who looked very sexy in a white shirt which had been left open at the throat, his dark hair and eyes an enticing contrast. He truly had no idea what this ensemble did to women, which made it all the more alluring.

The trip to Muskegon was easy enough, but then there was the interminable wait in line in order to fill out the required forms for his business license. Once that was done, he found a printing company he had looked up on the Internet, which, according to their website, promised to 'handle all of his business needs.' He had originally planned to make the rounds of a few mortgage companies, but decided it was best if he had his business cards ready to hand out first, and a portfolio of his work to present. So with business behind him, he headed back to Whitehall to go to the grocery store. He was going to cook the best Italian dinner Ivy had ever had, using his grandma's old-world recipes.

While all of this was going on, Ivy continued with her chores, and then began to pack an overnight bag with lightweight cotton pajamas and robe. She knew he would keep the house warm for Buddy; thin and sexy was pushing it and she wasn't ready to let him see her in her flannels, yet. Lightweight cotton bottoms and a matching tee seemed the better choice. By 4:30 she had everything Buddy or she could want; her son had been a little fussy in the morning, but after his nap he was a perfect baby, allowing his mother to get prepared without stress.

Ivy arrived at the door at 5:00 on the dot. The smells coming from inside were causing her mouth to water. She rang the bell and waited a second or two, before the door was opened by Fox who was dressed casually in jeans, a Lions tee shirt, and an apron. In Ivy's eyes, he looked good enough to eat; she instantly forgot about the food, and began to reconsider her decision about the sleeping arrangement. Fox pulled her in, taking Buddy's carrier from her. After making a few baby talk words of greeting to his sons, he placed his carrier on the floor and took Ivy in his arms, crushing her to his body in a hug that quickly turned to a lingering kiss. She enjoyed every second of it, until Buddy's coos brought her back to her senses.

"Mmmm, something smells good. What's cooking?"

"I made an antipasto of cheese, salami, and olives for starters, and then we'll have an Italian pasta salad made with tomatoes, basil, olives, peppers, and rotini. We'll follow that with the main course -- my grandmother's manicotti recipe." Fox watched her shocked face. He loved cooking and was happy to surprise her with his talent.

"I had no idea you could cook like that. I'm so useless in the kitchen it's embarrassing. I buy lots of frozen meals and cook in the microwave."

He kissed her lightly. "If you'll let me, I'll change all of that; I'd love to teach you to cook."

"That would be very nice. I'd like that."

"Perfect! Oops, unhand me woman, I need to stir something."

The rest of the evening was indeed perfect. Fox poured a different wine with each course, and when the meal was through, Ivy cleared the dishes, while he played on the floor with his son. He was tireless in making sounds with his mouth and shaking toys in front of Buddy to make him laugh. Ivy loved to hear the belly laugh that Buddy produced. She didn't think her little guy had ever been happier. This daily routine with Fox was beginning to feel very comfortable, and she liked it – she liked it a lot.

"Oh, oh, someone has produced a stinky diaper," said Fox, plugging his nose.

Ivy wiped her hands. "I'll get it."

"No, let me. Not that I'll like it, but it has to be done. I can handle it. Don't worry."

Ivy turned on the dishwasher and wiped the table, while Fox did the baby duties. When he returned he found Ivy sitting in a chair, flipping through a fishing magazine. "Is this all of the reading material you have?"

He handed Buddy to his mother, and sat on the sofa. "Actually, I'm a big reader. I just never have any time when I'm here. All of my books are at my apartment. My next project is to build a bookcase, on the wall next to the fireplace – floor to ceiling and slightly recessed." He gestured toward the empty wall. His face lit up when he talked about this house and what he had done to it.

"You are a very special man, Fox. You're good with numbers, you're a carpenter, and a handyman, you fish, *and* you cook! That's a lot of talents."

"Don't forget, I'm very good at kissing," he said with an impish grin.

Ivy chuckled, "That you are. But seriously, why haven't you married already?"

"You know the answer. I never found anyone I wanted until you." There was silence for a moment. He studied her a moment, and then asked, "Have you made a decision about the arrangements tonight?"

Ivy looked at her hands, playing with a peridot ring that had been passed down from her grandmother Olivia, and when she looked back up she said, "You've made it very tempting for me to agree to what you're hoping for. It's obvious that was your plan. But I'm afraid, Fox, afraid that if we move too fast, the only one who will suffer, if it doesn't work out, is Buddy. I'm not willing to risk that yet. Are you?"

"I don't plan to make anything difficult for either of you. If something doesn't work out between us, I have made a vow to be a good dad for the rest of my life, no matter what. That's not up for discussion."

"I understand, and I agree not to cause any problem for you and Buddy, ever. So let's just take it one day at a time, okay? We've only been visiting you for a few days; it hasn't even been a week, yet. And honestly, I don't want to be a part of a package with Buddy. When I do settle down with a man, I want him to love *me*. Yes, Buddy will always come with me, but I have not been lucky with family relationships in my life. I need stability, and I can't risk having something I cherish fall apart again. I don't think I could take it."

"You're right, of course. I'm pushing too hard. I tend to do that sometimes when I see something I want. And I want you, separate and apart from Buddy." Fox paused, and then continued, "Is kissing still allowed? 'Cause I really do like the kissing."

He was rewarded with a giggle that was music to his ears. "Yes, kissing is still on the table. Now, let's get this fella to bed."

"Once he's settled, how about a movie and some dessert?"

"Dessert? Depends on what it is," she laughed.

"Tiramisu, but I must confess, it's not homemade; I purchased it from a deli."

"I can't expect you to know how to do everything, but you sure know how to get to a girl's chocolate and coffee-loving heart. Let's hurry up. I'm dying to dig in."

Chapter Twenty-nine

"This is heavenly. Absolute perfection," said Ivy, licking her lips. He loved to watch her eat, so careful and delicate, relishing every bit as only a true food lover would do. "What's the movie?"

"The Notebook."

"Oh no! You didn't."

"What do you mean? I've never seen it, but my sister said you would love it because all girls do. What's wrong? Don't you like it?"

"Well, let's just say, before we start you'd better get me a box of Kleenex. How's your manliness? Because you might shed a tear or two, yourself."

Fox laughed out loud. "Not might -- will. I'm a softy when watching romantic movies. Oh, that rat -- my sister knew what she was doing. She planned it all;

I can see it now. Good thing I'm confident with who I am. I'm not afraid to admit that I'm in touch with my feminine side, and I won't mind a bit if you see me sniffle a little."

Fox put the DVD in the player, and they settled in for one of the best love stories ever written. Ivy snuggled next to Fox, and when they were finished with their dessert, they wrapped up in an afghan like two lovers who had been together a long time. Ivy was so comfortable and happy with the way the evening was going. She was glad she had agreed to stay the night.

When the movie was over, Fox wiped her tears and held her close. He whispered, "Have you changed your mind about what room you want to stay in?"

"I would love nothing better than to go back on my decision, but I'm going to be good. The guest room it is."

"Well, I can't say I'm not disappointed. I thought the movie and the tiramisu would clinch the deal. But I do have a proposition."

"What's that," she said sleepily.

"How about if I keep Buddy here tomorrow, and you go home. You can have some free time to shop or read or whatever you want. Wait a minute -- hear me out. I can see you hesitating. But listen, I can handle it, and you'll only be a few minutes away. If I need you I'll call."

"I suppose."

"Okay, good, but there's more. See if you can get Nancy to take over the baby duties at about six or seven. I'll bring him to you, and then I'll take you out for a real date. We've never gone on one, other than a rained-out picnic and lunch at the diner. What do you say?"

"Wow! That does sound nice. A real date, huh? Dressed up and everything?"

"Yes, we'll dress up. I know of a great steak place. Maybe we can even get in a dance or two."

"Oh, Fox. That would really be nice. I don't know the last time I went on a nighttime dinner date with a man. I'm embarrassed to say it's been several years, and if I recall, it didn't end well, at that."

"Wonderful. I'll be sure to make this a good memory for you. We need more time alone without worrying about that little guy in the next room waking up. And I have something important to talk about, too."

"We could talk now. Nothing's stopping us."

"No, I want to save it. You'll see why tomorrow."

Ivy raised an eyebrow. "My, aren't you mysterious."

"Mysterious is the perfect word." As he kissed her lovingly, he could feel his restraint dissolving. "Now, time for bed, before I'm unable to control myself any longer."

They parted at her bedroom door. She was about to ask him in, but he stepped away and left her, and the moment was gone.

Buddy slept through the night but woke up extremely early. That was something Fox was not prepared for, but Ivy let him handle everything, while she stood silently by in case Fox got into trouble. Maybe things didn't go quite as smoothly as when his mother got him ready for the day, but Buddy didn't seem to notice. Fox was still awkward with bath time, but Buddy had fun with his father, splashing and making an overall mess of the place, and Fox loved every minute of it. Ivy just shook her head.

After breakfast and when she was sure it was safe to go, she left the two alone for the rest of the day. "I want you to promise me that if anything goes wrong, you'll call right away. I won't mind a bit coming back here, if he starts to cry and you can't get him to stop. Promise?"

"Okay, okay, but don't worry so much. We'll be fine. Now, go and have fun. Do your hair or any other girlie thing you like. We'll be there to pick you up about 6."

Fox had loved seeing Ivy's messy look in the morning – no makeup, tousled hair, sleepy eyes. It was very sexy, and he had been so turned on it was difficult to keep his mind on his son. While dressing for the day, he had had to stay clear of the loose floor board, which was almost torture for him. Tonight, if all went his way, it would be worth it.

Mother was kissing her child over and over again. It was next to impossible for her to tear herself away, but once Fox took her in his arms and began his own kissing, she relented. 'Maybe I *have* been over-protective,' she thought.

The day dragged on for Ivy; she kept glancing at the clock all day long. She showered and then left to get her hair done and followed that up with a mani/pedi. She bought a new dress at that cute little boutique that recently opened, and then picked up a new shade of lipstick. The taupe-colored sheath dress highlighted her hair and brought out the color of her eyes; the neckline dipped suggestively low showing the curve of her breasts. The new light tangerine lip gloss enhanced her creamy complexion. When she viewed herself in the mirror, running her hands over her hips, she said,

"What man wouldn't want this?" Then she laughed happily, hoping for the best results tonight.

When the doorbell rang at 6, Ivy flew to open it so she could get her arms around her darling son. She had missed him terribly, and had felt lost all day long without him nearby. Now that she was holding him again, she was reluctant to leave.

Fox was very proud of himself for being able to handle the child all day by himself. He was amazed to see how Ivy had missed Buddy so much, and knew already that he would feel the same if Buddy were not in his life on a regular basis.

Nancy arrived to take over the baby duties, and once again Buddy just went with the flow. He loved people, and like a friendly little puppy dog, he didn't really care who he was with as long as it was someone who loved him.

Once Fox and Ivy had closed the door behind them, Fox pulled her into his arms and whispered, "You look gorgeous tonight. I wanted to say so earlier, but you were a little occupied with our son."

"Sorry. I missed him so much. I've never been away from him so long before. It was much harder than I expected."

Fox caressed her arms, then kissed her tenderly. "Let's get out of here before you change your mind." Then he walked her to his pickup truck. "Sorry about the ride. I didn't bring the Miata with me. It was only meant to be a one-day trip to sell the house. I had no idea what was in store for me."

"Or me, either."

The date was perfect as far as Ivy was concerned. A perfect meal with a perfect guy. They held hands in between bites. The wine added to the mood and after a few glasses they decided to stop drinking so it would be safe to drive home. Once their table was cleared, they got up to dance to a slow song, and Fox held Ivy tightly in his arms. He knew what was coming next, but she had no idea. He was excited but a little fearful at the same time. And then finally, the time was right to bring up his suggestion.

As they danced and he held her closely to his chest, he said softly, "Will you go home with me now? I need to tell you something."

Ivy looked up at him and asked, "Can't we go back to my place and relieve Nancy?"

"I'd rather not; besides I talked to Nancy when you were getting your coat. She hinted that time was not an issue, even if it was to be overnight. I know—I know what you said, but you have to hear me out, and it's important we go to the cottage."

"I don't understand, but I'll only go there for a little while. Do you want to leave now?"

"I can't think of anything I'd rather do." He kissed her right there on the dance floor, and she melted into his sweet affection.

They were quiet on the drive to Wabaningo; Ivy was not sure what was happening, but she trusted Fox now, and she was eager to spend more time with him. A crescent-moon hung in the clear sky; the light coming from it was so bright it looked like it had been backlit by a spotlight. Ivy put her head on the backrest and watched the stars up above as they traveled to her great-grandmother's home, thinking about the times Ruby and Sal would have taken this same road over one hundred years ago.

When they arrived Fox suddenly seemed nervous. He fussed with some candles and then he lit the fireplace. He purposely chose not to turn on the electric lights. The glow of the flames produced a feeling of warmth and comfort; Ivy had never been happier. Fox led her to the couch and then got them each a glass of Chardonnay, and although Ivy felt she really didn't need another glass of wine, she accepted it because Fox was so eager to please. Her head was a little buzzy, but it was a good buzz. Every muscle in her body was relaxed, and as she watched him move around the house, she had a chance to take in his fine form and tight muscles. He was a wonderful figure of a man; not too many women had a chance to spend time with someone with his good looks. She sighed and closed her eyes, and when she felt the cushions next to her move, she realized she had dozed off for a second. Opening her eyes and slowly peeking out, she discovered Fox seated closely next to her. He pulled her to him, putting his arm around her as they leaned back together. Then he kissed her with the passion he had been holding in all evening.

"Ivy, Ivy, I'm so glad you're back in my life," he whispered. "Do you understand what all of this means to me? You and my son? I don't think anything has ever been this important – this is life changing. I've been flying high since you first told me about Buddy."

"I'm glad you took it so well. I've been worried about your reaction for over a year."

"It's all so perfect that I don't want to ruin anything, but I have to confess that I, too, have a secret."

"You do?" She sat up to look at him, but he gently pushed her back against his chest. He had a lot to say, and he preferred not to be looking at her when he did.

"Will you listen to me and try not to be judgmental?" When she nodded, he went on. "First of all, I want to tell you that when I read Ruby and Sal, I was elated. I was surprised at what a wonderful story it was, and I was thrilled that you had actually fulfilled your dream. But there was something else that was shocking about that book. The whole story about the ruby necklace was mystical and beautiful, and to anyone else reading it, it was just a fantasy. But this is where things get complicated."

"Why is that?" she asked, now more curious than anything else. The rumble of his voice through his chest was so soothing; she waited for him to go on with his story.

"Well, remember when I first came into the house, before it went up for auction?"

"Yes, that's the day I began to mistrust you. We had a big fight."

"That's right. You had come up from the cellar and found me there in the kitchen. You thought I had been using you to get to the house because it was part of Prohibition and had belonged to Al Capone."

"Yes, but I was wrong, wasn't I." she said in a dreamlike daze.

"You were, because I loved you so much already and never had any intention of hurting you. I didn't even know at that time that it was your great-grandmother's house. I was just there to do an appraisal."

"Mm-hmm. I know that now."

"And then afterward, after I had won the house in the auction, you wouldn't speak to me. I couldn't reach you. I tried and tried, and then I finally gave up."

"That was stupid of me. I've never behaved like that before." Ivy sat up and kissed him to try to make up for her childish behavior.

"Well, one day, I was in the bedroom and the loose board squeaked. When I pried it up, I realized that that was most likely a hiding spot for money; but of course, it was empty. Then suddenly I remembered how flustered you were when you came up those stairs. I knew you had been down there searching for something, and so I ran down and began my own search. I didn't know what I expected to find, but I did finally find something – something very important. I've been saving it for you."

"You did? You have?" Now Ivy sat up fully, so she could watch his face as he told the rest.

"I want you to understand I never had any intention of keeping it. I just couldn't find the right time to give it to you, and when I suddenly found myself engaged, I didn't know what to do with it." Fox stood up, slowly separating himself from her, and then he went into the bedroom. He lifted the board and pulled out the package. He had placed it in a small velvet drawstring bag he had found in a gift shop instead of the bulky box.

Ivy's eyes widened with surprise as he withdrew the ruby and diamond necklace. Ruby's very own necklace! The one Sal had given to her on her sixteenth birthday. The one he had hidden in order to protect it from the Federal agents. He held it up, and the candle light made the jewels sparkle and dance. Fox's arm was tingling with a fierceness he had never felt from it before, and as he placed it around Ivy's neck, he could have sworn it hummed.

Ivy's entire body was suddenly ablaze with passion. She began to see images of the past -- Ruby and Sal, Max and Maisy, and even Edward and Clara. She cried for them, and she cried for herself. She was relieved and ecstatic at the same time. "My grandmother's necklace. It's all true. It *is* real! It's real! Oh, Fox, I don't care why you kept it from me, all I care about is that I have it. It meant so much to Ruby for me to find it."

Fox felt safe enough to take her in his arms once again. She was not going to reject him, as he had feared. He kissed her with a powerful desire neither one had ever felt before. It was wild and crazy; their flames wanted to be doused, they needed to be doused. They ran their hands over each other's bodies, trying to touch every inch at once. They could not bear to tear their lips away, but the need to kiss every area of exposed skin was imperative. They were suddenly out of control, over the moon, and at a sexual height they had not thought possible. The couch could not hold their writhing bodies. Fox carried Ivy to the bedroom, never once releasing their kiss. Then they fell to the bed, and forgot about everything else but the two of them. Fulfilling their desires was all that mattered; they could not have stopped if they had wanted to at this point. It was the culmination of one hundred and twenty eight years of the bejeweled aphrodisiac, since Edward had first felt the rubies placed in his hands by the gypsy woman. The rubies and diamonds were home once again where they belonged, and they were on fire.

When the couple was sated, they lay in each other's arms, amazed at what had just taken place. Fox turned and positioned himself so he was lying face to face with Ivy; their noses almost touching. He trailed his fingers from her shoulder to the dip of her waist and back up on the curve of her hips. She shivered, still sensitive to his touch.

"Ivy, my darling, my sweet girl, you are the love of my life. It's obvious we are meant to be together. I love you with every beat of my heart."

"I love you, too. I always have," declared Ivy. "There wasn't one single night that I didn't dream of you, but I was so angry that I denied it even to myself. But Fox, there is one thing that bothers me. What if you hadn't found the necklace? Or what if you gave it to someone else? Would you feel that passion for that woman, too?"

"You need to know something very important," he whispered. "I've never had another woman here, in this house, except my sisters and mother."

"Not Mandy?" Ivy was surprised.

"She asked several times to come to see my cottage, but I knew it wouldn't be right. Besides when you were out of my life, the rubies were cold. They lost their fire, until you came back into the house. Strange, isn't it?"

"Well, that fits in with the stories. I guess it's all true, then. I wasn't sure about that part."

"What do you mean?" he said kissing her nose.

She kissed him on the lips before going ahead with the story. "I can't wait for you to read the draft of Maisy and Max, because the oddest thing happened." She went on to describe to him about the night she had attended the Buster Keaton Film Festival, her meeting with a strange woman named Gina, and then another meeting with her fourth cousin Veronica who was a direct descendant of a man named Max. "Her story was the reason I wrote the second book. I knew the necklace was real, because I actually saw a picture of it on Ruby's mother. But I was never truly sure of the magical powers it held until tonight. Once you read the book, you'll see how the necklace seems to find its way to the men who then give it to women who are in a direct ancestry line. So it was given first to a woman named Clara by Edward, then their son Max gave it to Maisy, then even though it was thought to be lost forever in Chicago, through a bizarre set of circumstances, it worked its way from Sal to Ruby. Since it was lost in this house, it skipped my grandmother Olivia, and my own mother."

"Maybe they never found their perfect matches – their soul mates."

"That sounds about right."

"You see, Ivy, when I held it in the basement, I instinctively knew it was meant for you. But not just for you alone. It was meant for *us*. Will you move in with me and be a family with Buddy? I guess, what I'm trying to say is will you marry me? Will you be my wife, and spend the rest of your days with me? I want to dance under the stars with you while you're wearing the rubies. I want to make love to you in front of the fireplace. I want to hold you and kiss you when you're hurt, and I want to celebrate with you when you're happy. I love you beyond all reason."

"And if I say yes, will our story be that you proposed to me while we were naked in bed?"

"Yes, if you say yes, I will never deny my love for you, or where or how we fell in love."

Ivy laughed. "Then I say yes. Yes!!!"

"We'll go to your apartment and begin to move you in today. Too soon?"

"Not soon enough." And with that declaration, the rubies danced, sparkled, and hummed for joy. The couple didn't leave the room for several hours more.

$$\approx$$

"Fox," Ivy said dreamily, "make sure I never wear this necklace in public. We would disgrace ourselves."

He laughed with a sexy chuckle at the thought, and then added, "Just think, Ivy, you're back in the cottage in the same bed as Ruby and Sal, doing the same thing they did. It's exactly where you belong. And someday, when the time is right, we'll pass it on to Buddy. Of course, he'll be grown and be known as Sal Marzetti then."

"My baby? Doing this? Lord help us. But if it's true that for some reason we have been chosen, then we must keep up the tradition," she said with twinkling eyes. "Because maybe we'll pass it on to our *daughter's* suitor, if a dark-haired man with flashing eyes comes calling."

"My daughter? Not my little girl! And let it be known that I plan to use this until I'm old and grey. And if we are still hot for each other when the grown-up Sal has found the woman we think is right, then keep in mind, we were doing just fine on our own the weekend that Buddy was conceived. We'll have nothing to worry about." Then he toppled her on her back, and the lovers enjoyed each other once more.

Epilogue

Nancy was over the moon when she heard the news that Ivy and Fox were engaged and moving in together. She said she would miss having Ivy next door, but with the new baby coming she and Matt had already discussed moving, anyway. He had already started looking at lake properties. It was a possibility they could be neighbors again.

Ivy gifted Nancy with every piece of baby furniture she had. It was only seven months old, and Fox had just purchased duplicates of everything. Nancy was so happy, she cried. What a savings on the budget, she said.

It took several days and many trips before the couple was firmly established in the cottage. With the help of Matt, Fox was able to carry the bigger pieces they wanted to keep; the rest would go in storage until they could sell it in the spring.

Winter was moving in quickly with an early snowfall; the first delicate flakes had appeared already to give them a taste of what was to come. The smell of snow in the air was refreshing and clean, and as it covered the fallen leaves with its soft white blanket, it made the world look pristine and virginal. It was the same way Ivy and Fox felt about their newfound relationship – fresh and new.

While Buddy bounced in his chair on the floor next to them, Fox and Ivy curled up in each other's arms on the couch; Ivy watched their son play while Fox read her 'Maisy and Max' manuscript. Her son was such a joy. Ivy thanked God for all of the wonderful things that had happened to her in the last month and more so in the last year. She never thought she could feel so fulfilled and loved.

"Ivy, I hope you are going to continue with your writing," he said, as he finished reading the final page of the first draft of 'Maisy and Max.' This is amazing. You're very good."

"I do plan to write, but I don't know where to go next. Obviously, we'll never know any more to this story than what we already do. I took Edward back to 1889. That's based on everything I had learned from Ronnie. I doubt if anyone knows any more than that. Besides I wouldn't know where to begin. If it hadn't been for Buster Keaton's connection to Muskegon and Bluffton, I might not be here with you today."

"You'll figure it out. Your relatives *are* pretty *unforgettable*. Who knows what will happen next."

Ivy sighed contentedly, and then smiled to herself, "Yes, who knows."

Continue the story of Fox and Ivy in

Ivy and Fox, Book 3

of The Unforgettables

View an excerpt following Author's Notes

Author's Notes

Thank you for reading Maisy and Max. I hope you enjoyed it. This book took a few turns even I had not expected. As in most of my books the characters seem to take on a life of their own and sometimes drive the story in places I could not have foreseen.

I began with the idea of doing a love story based around Muskegon and the Buster Keaton connection, all of which is true. Muskegon does have an area called Bluffton on Muskegon Lake, and Buster Keaton's family actually did have a summer cottage there. My grandfather talked about knowing Buster as a young man. Buster loved to play baseball with locals whenever his family came to town for the summer. I've often wondered if my grandfather was one of the boys who played ball with him. Buster loved Bluffton and always proclaimed Muskegon as his hometown. (It is mine also; as a matter of fact, I am a member of a Muskegon County Pioneer Family with 8 generations born or residing in Muskegon) Buster would practice his prat falls and routines and create some new sketches and tricks right there on the docks and the beach, and then try them out for the locals. As more vaudevillians (over 200 each season) began to come to town, an Actor's Colony was formed, and it is this group that is celebrated to this day every October with the Buster Keaton Convention sponsored by the Damfinos. For more information go to www.busterkeaton.com.

The beautiful Frauenthal Theater in downtown Muskegon on Western Avenue is the site of the annual film festival. When I was growing up it was known as the Michigan Theater, and is as one of the most beautiful theaters in the state. The Frauenthal has held the Miss Michigan Scholarship Pageant since 1950, as well as many other events and concerts. Each October several Buster Keaton films are shown to the accompaniment of live organ music. In front of it is where you will see a lovely bronze statue of Buster Keaton looking through the camera, as he was not only celebrated for his stunts and acting but was also world renown as one of the best directors of all time.

Descriptions of Muskegon in that time period are accurate as far as the beach and activities at Lake Michigan. The Barnum and Bailey circus truly did come to town regularly; I found their schedule posted on the Internet and based the dates of arrival for Edward and Clara on that list. The date that Edward and Clara were in London with the circus is also factual, but of course, Edward and Clara are not.

I had originally planned this book to begin with a Buster Keaton fan sitting in the Frauenthal Theater where she would meet her love interest. It was never meant to be a continuation of Ivy and Fox's story, but a separate story on its own. Little did I know that when Ivy sat down in the plush seats waiting for a viewing of The General to begin that a strange old woman would take the seat next to her, thus taking Ivy on a genealogical mystery that changed the young woman's life forever. I swear to you, Gina came out of nowhere and shocked me. I said to myself, 'Now, why didn't I think of that? Oh that's right, I just did!'

I hope you'll continue the journey with *Book Three of The Unforgettables,* called *Ivy and Fox.* There are more genealogical mysteries yet to come as the ruby necklace travels through time always seeking its rightful owner.

Please leave a review of this book and others you have read at Amazon.com or Goodreads.com. It's a big help with my author rankings. Thank you.

Here are some more links for you:

http://www.actorscolony.com/Maps.htm

http://www.actorscolony.com/lmp.htm

http://frauenthal.org/

http://www.circushistory.org/Routes/PTB.htm

Ivy and Fox

Prologue – Ukraine, 1868

Anya was lying flat on her back, gazing at the sky. The damp grass was beginning to soak through her dress, but she didn't care. She wore many layers of garment, and it would be a while before the dampness reached her skin. This was her favorite time of the day, when the sun dipped below the horizon but left enough light behind to see her surroundings which now colored in a blue haze.

The stars were exceptionally clear tonight; she wished she knew more about the constellations. She had been told the stars formed to make pictures and each picture had a name, but without any formal schooling she could only guess at what others saw. She tried to make pictures of her own by imagining lines drawn from one star to another, but all she could create were triangles and squares. 'So much for my creativity,' she thought.

Sasha snuggled in beside her, but always the working dog, she kept her eyes scanning the flock. Her warmth felt good and was a comfort to the young woman all alone on the hillside of the Carpathian Mountains. This was the most dangerous time of day for them all. Predators were everywhere; the dog was essential to life. The sheep quietly bleated, calling each other to make sure their lambs were nearby and safe. Sasha settled in for a few moments of sleep, knowing that Anya was alert. The dog's job began when the darkness was so black that only a canine could see through it. Once Anya fell asleep, the loyal sheepdog would move quietly among the flock throughout the night to make sure all was well. It was the only way

Anya could get any rest. If she returned to the village in the valley herding fewer sheep than she had gone up the mountain with, there would be consequences that she could not bear to think about. Her father was a hard task master, because the sheep were their only livelihood. They were to be protected at all costs.

Anya had been coming up the mountain from her Ukrainian village every summer since she turned thirteen, and nothing horrible had ever happened, but she was warned each time she left that there was always a first time, so she must be alert. Anya would spend two whole weeks in the grasslands all by herself, with no one but her dog and nothing to protect herself with but her skinning knife, and bow and arrow. The first time she came here, when she was twelve, she only stayed for one week, but then she was with her older brother. He taught her everything she needed to know to care for the flock, but her brother was gone now. He lost his life in a tragic accident when he fell off the hay wagon and broke his neck. The other brothers and sisters had all married; they had their own families to take care of now, so it was up to her to keep the family flock strong and healthy. The way things were going, she would be responsible for the flock for years to come, and would most likely become an old maid, the only child left to care for Mama and Papa. Anya was already nineteen years old, and so far there were no prospects of marriage. It was beginning to be an embarrassment for her parents.

Anya was quite beautiful, with an oval face, large blue eyes, and a clear rosy complexion, thanks to the fresh mountain air. Her cheekbones were high and prominent, framed by her hair sandy brown hair which she always kept neatly braid and wrapped around her head. The problem was her personality. She could be quite judgmental at times, and sharp of tongue. She knew she should try to soften her ideas, but none of the men or young boys in the village suited her fancy, and she refused to marry until one of them did. The list of eligible men was short, and unless she wanted to marry a cousin or an old man, – which might happen if Papa had anything to say about it – she would end up a spinster. Recently there had been talk of her marrying Leonid Pavlovich, but he was already fifty, with gray hair and a round fat belly. Papa said he had plenty of money, a large farm, and a substantial herd of cattle. It would be a good alliance for the family, but Anya would rather die than consent to that arrangement. Maybe there would be a sign in the stars tonight that would tell her what to do. Papa had said he would not force her, but she knew if she didn't agree to the marriage, the rest of their lives would be difficult, and she would feel guilty. Times were tough. The Russians, the Austrians, and the Polish all wanted a piece of the lush farmlands of Ukraine. 'Won't they ever leave us alone and in peace?' she thought. 'Don't we deserve our own homeland like everyone else?'

Anya linked her fingers tightly together and began a prayer to God to show her the way. "Please, Father, let my people live in peace. Let my family be rich with food, and help me to make the right decision for my life, for myself and for Mama and Papa. I will put it all into your hands if you will only show me the way. Please give me a sign if you believe that I should marry Leonid." Anya waited for a full five minutes in silence, all the while with her hands folded together. There was nothing, no sounds at all but a few night bird calls. Then Anya whispered, "Please, Lord, tell me if you have someone saved for me. Show me that you have my life planned out, and I will follow where you lead." At that exact moment a shooting star crossed the heavens. It was so bright, Anya could see the entire field before her. Tears came to her eyes. He had heard her! God had listened to her plea. She kissed her rosary, always so near to her heart, and then made the sign of the cross, saying, "Thank you, Lord. In the name of the Father, the Son, and the Holy Ghost. Amen."

"Did you see that Sasha? We are going to be okay. God has something wonderful planned for us. Something we could never foresee or make happen on our own. I can't wait to find out what it is -- or *who* it is." She clapped her hands together with excitement and then laughed aloud as Sasha licked her face while thumping his tail at his master's joy.

Made in the USA
Monee, IL
02 December 2020